Duskwood

A. WOLF

Duskwood
Copyright © 2022 A. Wolf
Published by A. Wolf
ISBN:978-1-7397666-2-7
First edition: January 2022

COVER DESIGN:
A. Wolf

To Eloise and the Argonauts, for showing me a better world.

I: KINDLING

1

I HEAR IT CALLING. Now is the time to run.

My mother's face is turned away, towards Liesl. There are others—the pallid, muttering women—but the only eyes on me are those of the fish, half-gutted and bulging in my hands.

The sea is churning on the grey shore. I can taste salt, and feel it too, pressed into my skin and my eyes. The wind is a beating monolith, a beast with no soul.

I spy my mother one last time. My heart begins to shake against my chest and the seconds slow before me. *Yes. Now is the time to run.*

My boots hit the sand and the world snaps back to speed; the shore slides and sprays in a murky mist as I go. Tinged with excitement, the salt wind becomes my partner, and my heart roars with the crashing waves.

"Kestra!" The shout is muffled by everything in the air, and by the blood rushing in my ears, greater than any ocean. I can't tell whose voice it is that yelled—no matter; right now, the men are gone. Though they'll try, none of them can catch me. And so my heart lurches with the freedom of the chase. Air sings past me; my hair swirls back in tangled bliss, and I know in one bright moment that this is what birds feel when they fly.

My feet smack hard against cold rock and the shock of the vibrations through my bones make me human again—but the dancing fire within me rages on.

I steal a glance behind me. A handful of drab figures swarm in the distance, fast and angry like ants. With a gulp of delight, I come to the main path, made a river of roiling mud by the Spring rains. Houses line the way from the shore in a growing labyrinth of sturdy stone and old thatch, and the sky bears down on it all, thick and grey. Far away, the wood peeks out at me past the houses and the gate and the fields, whispering.

Clotted and footprint-strewn, the mud of the path grasps at my boots; I push ahead, harder, but it fights me. My lungs are crashing into one another and an ache is beginning to build in my heavy legs. I fix my shuddering gaze; all there is is this path. I may slow, but I will make it.

Then I'm almost thrown forwards as my boot sticks fast, lodged under some cursed, sunken stone in the unforgiving sludge. Desperate, angry heat burns through my core. *No. Not after I've come this far.*

Yet now I hear their pounding feet closer behind me, and I can't help but imagine the sound of their reprimands. The end is so close. The *beginning.* My stomach jolts. A hand grasps my shoulder, harsh as a claw. It's Mother, worn and panting, seething as the Rhenesee.

"You *fool,*" she spits, words sputtering between ragged breaths. A guilty, rebellious spark jumps inside me, setting my fear alight. I stumble triumphantly to the edge of the wood—feeling like a weary traveller, returning after many years—I let myself breathe out. The sweeping joy that hits me at seeing the faint firelights of Hanshen is not something I ever thought I'd feel.

Overwhelmed, I stare out from the boundary, engulfed in a sudden expanse of scattered stars. Beneath them all, Hanshen flickers, small against the titans of sea and sky. Tiny against the wood, which encircles its fields like a gargantuan wall.

Upon the shore lie the black shadows of boats, long-docked. Something heavy looms again in my soul. Florian and the others have returned. He's worried, and Mother is furious—in my bones, I know it. Yet my body longs for a bed to sleep in and walls to keep out the cold salt of the wind... I have to return. There is no other place; there is no other choice.

Perhaps if I slip into the house in secret, her rage will have faded by the morning.

2

I am a shadow. The edges of the village path are my domain. I duck beneath the lights of the windows, waiting for them to be snuffed out. The streets are bare; the houses are quiet. Hanshen soon sleeps, but something in me is trembling, as though I am being pulled towards certain doom.

I sneak carefully to my family's home, at the western end of the village. There is no light. I consider climbing the stones of the wall, and sneaking through the wooden shutters of the first floor —but they creak, perhaps even worse than the door, so it can't be worth the effort. Then again, it would only be Florian to hear them... and Liesl. I can't forget her. I wince to imagine her waking —realisation followed by shrill clamouring for Mother. No. I might as well use the door.

Approaching the front of the house, I give the Lord's Turn a nod of mutual understanding. It's not carved very well, clumsily scraped into the stone above the door, but I hope Rhene can see.

I keep my breathing as quiet as I can, tensing my stomach.

Gingerly, I pry open the rough wood of the door, cradling it. In anticipation, I wince again, ready for a screeching creak to echo through the house.

There's a little metallic whine as the door comes open, but that's all. My breath sags out of me and my muscles finally relax. *Everything's alright.* I step into the main room. It's shrouded in shadow, but can I imagine where everything is without trying: the table, laced with patterns I scratched into its underside years ago during a particularly boring dinner; six chairs, two for guests, one with arms—Father's, and the fireplace, blackened with soot. There isn't much else.

I glance over to the door of my parents' bedroom, illuminated in a sliver of moonlight. It's soundly shut. Relief is flooding my body like a soft, calming spring. Silently, I pad into the room and close the door carefully behind me.

A light springs awake in the darkness. The sudden change jolts me. I see Mother's face, hard and grim. She sits upright before a candle.

"Kestra," she says, and her voice is not angry. Just cold. I step forward, heavy. I've done my share of running today.

"Do you have anything to say?" she asks. She looks tired. Not just wrapped in the tiredness of the night, but with a dullness of the eyes that makes me want to ask if everything's alright.

But I don't ask. We have an agreement, as opposites; an unspoken pact of mutual dislike. Anyway, she's tired because of me, not anything else—because I ran from the Path, in the most obvious way possible. The rest of the village saw me go. That's a painful thing for her, having an unruly daughter. An unmarriable daughter. She's never said it, but I know it's true.

"I'm sorry." I say, because I am. Not for the adventure, for the wonder of the woods, but for the running away to get there. "I mean it this time."

Her expression doesn't shift. There's her thinking face, brow wrinkles and all. A verdict is coming.

"We thought you might not come back." she murmurs. Something about the way she says it irks me. Without meaning to, my thoughts are snagged, caught into the shape of words.

"Would you have liked that?" I respond.

She hesitates softly, taken aback, but too calm. Too accepting of the idea.

"Don't say things like that, Kestra." she breathes, looking so exhausted that I feel a pang in my chest and almost want to take everything back. She sighs. "I should tell the Speaker to lock you in the Hold for this—it would show you some discipline. Rhene knows I've lacked it."

She hasn't lacked it. Not at all. I remember the ache of bruises on my arms when I was smaller. But the thought of the Hold, dank, black and salty with dregs of the shore... It's only punishment for the worst of blasphemies. A part of me trembles slightly.

Mother doesn't continue. She just stares into the candle flame. I go to sit down, making sure to avoid my father's chair—no one can sit in it, not even when he's not in the room. She makes sure of it. We sit there together, unspeaking, words fragmenting in the air between us but never truly forming. Eventually, she speaks again.

"Go to bed, Kestra. Tomorrow is the holy day."

Her voice has a little of something questioning in it, strangely unsure of herself, though at this hour I don't think she'll double back on it—sleep is the star in both of our minds right now. She shuffles to the bedroom door with her candle.

I don't let the release of tension overwhelm me with peace. Somehow, I'll be made to pay, I know it. So when I climb the ladder to our makeshift second floor, I try not to wake Florian. There isn't much triumph to revel in.

Without light, I silently find my way to my space and curl into the blankets. I hear rain begin to patter on the roof; the wind howls outside, more than the roiling of a normal sea wind. I smell a storm. I taste it, curled up in the shell of our hollow attic. My head buzzes with nothing, and I toss and turn, trying my best to roll into sleep.

I see them. Bright cities; rivers of ice; sooty, bustling streets. Fuzzy, shifting, radiating light in the way only dreams can. They are Florian's stories, given unnatural life.

Yet there is the wood again, mossy and dark with night. Even as a maze of shivering shadow, it calls me back. Though it sits before me in every detail, I forget my fear.

When I come awake, the house is too grey and dark, riddled with irritating clarity. I want to smooth it out, to make it soft.

Florian's shaking me. "What were you thinking?!" he exclaims.

His face is set in an exasperated smile, but there are tremors in it. He holds me close. I wrap my arms around him.

"Sorry." My voice is rough with the morning, rubbed with restless sleep. Even in this state, though, I know not to speak of the strange call from the wood: "I was just... so bored."

He doesn't respond, just sighs. A spark of annoyance jumps to my throat. I pull away and look him in the face.

"If you were forced to gut fish and sweep floors day in and day out, you'd want an adventure too."

Discomfort pinches his expression. I imagine what it's like for him—out on the waves most days, out in the unknown North. Sometimes even down to Brennof, on the blue moons when catch is particularly blessed. Hot envy, like bubbling acid, aches and boils within me. I look away.

"Kestra," Florian says, patting me on the shoulder, "being out there can be boring, too." He chuckles a little. "Spending a whole day with Father, every day? He's a man of few words."

I huff, getting to my feet. "Well, maybe one day I can pretend to be a boy. Then no one will be afraid of me being near a ship anymore."

Florian smiles ruefully. "One day. And until then, I'll tell you all the stories you want."

We go downstairs together. Liesl is already with mother, getting her hair braided. Father stands in the corner, silent.

The trek to the Lord's Chapel is a short one, but we walk slowly, caught in the buzzing aftershock of last night's storm. Mother and Father share solemn greetings with those around us as all of Hanshen begins to congregate on the main path. We are a dull river flowing towards the cliff.

Eyes follow me until I glance back at them—then they shift away like startled fish. People's faces are filled with everything: guilty curiosity, quiet disdain, surprise at my still being here. I don't care. Why should *they*? I'm back on the Path—I only left for a little bit, anyway.

Amidst the hushed talk, Florian fulfils his promise, whispering a story he once heard from a merchant in Brennof.

"In the East, they say there are dragons hidden in mountains and deep, dark caves. In Cer'ah, people leave offerings to them, sort of like we do for Lord Rhene, and in return—"

Mother shushes him. "Focus on the Lord, Florian."

He knows better than to speak again, so we continue wordlessly.

I see the silence of the young here, made drab and dull-eyed. There are the boys I haven't spoken to for years, taken by the daily pull of the sea. There are the girls that languish with me amongst buckets of fish guts, who talk about anything and everything they can get away with before being shut up again, ever-tethered to their homes. It all feels lifeless; there's something wrong, but I don't know what it is.

We make it to the entrance. The procession treads through an old archway of salt-stained stone, relegating themselves evenly to pew upon pew. As the crowd begins to settle like a faintly murmuring sea, the Speaker emerges from his shadowed passage. I feel the hushed reverence wash over us. There is silence in the Chapel, save the howling of the morning wind. It echoes freely over our heads—this place has no roof. Here, I always feel exposed.

The Speaker raises his wrinkled hand. He wears a grey robe, and the Lord's Turn hangs heavy about his neck. Mother always argues that he is not as old as he appears. She says his wisdom has aged him, and we must listen.

He speaks of our Lord, our Father of the sea, voice dry as sand. I can't stop staring at his puckering, wind-pale skin.

I listen hard nonetheless. I want to feel Lord Rhene in my heart, but the only sensation I receive is like a stone, cold at the bottom of my chest. Flashes of green, of moss and clear, bubbling water intersperse the pale greyness that I cling to. I blink again and again, trying desperately to clear it.

"What lies at the borders of our Lord's Path is misery and punishment," he intones, gazing up to the bare sky as though confirming the truth with Rhene himself. Real or not, I feel the weight of eyes on me.

"By the eternal currents of the sea, we were made to serve Him. To repay." At that, I can't help but stifle a sigh. I can't remember how many times this story has been told. I glance at Mother. She hasn't noticed my displeasure. Her face is full with the spirit of the sea, anxious for him to go on.

"Our ancestors were punished by our Lord Father, set to be drowned in the depths of his domain. Yet we were saved by his grace." The Speaker makes the sign of the Turn before us. "Walk His Path—you men, the path of the follower, of serving him and receiving His bounty; you women, the path of the meek, of bearing more children to serve Him."

Whenever anybody speaks of bearing children, my breath can't help but catch in my throat. Something churns in my stomach, and I feel fleshy and fragile. Soon, they say. Soon you'll marry, and be happy. And have children. They'll be happy, too— to live under the merciful watch of our divine Father, Lord Rhene.

My eyes wander from the Speaker to the sea, caught in a small hollow window through the rock. They drift again, to Florian. Then they find Liesl, hand grasped in Mother's. I see their faces, made worn and grim by the rough light of the morning.

Are we happy?

I don't want to think about that. I stare at my piece of the sea.

"...beware of the witches, and the wild, sinful spirits from

. . .

Later, we coax her to dinner. She sits quietly, picking at her fish, while Mother makes conversation.

"What are you called?" she begins, trying her best to make her tone delicate, as though it's handling something fragile. The girl's dark eyes remain fixed on her food. There's something calm about her. She isn't scared, just thinking. She takes a bite, then glances up.

"Renate." she murmurs. *Renate. I've never heard of a name like that before.*

She goes back to her food. The atmosphere at our wordless table is like sludge. Of course, Mother decides to stir it.

"That's a lovely name," she says, smiling. Renate keeps eating. Mother pushes through and nods approvingly, thinking to herself for a moment.

"You'll make a wonderful wife to one of the boys here, when it's time." she says.

Renate stops, looks up. Though her face is drawn at first with murmurings of confusion, I watch her expression cool to a barely noticeable frostiness. She's realising something. Calculating.

Then she becomes blank, smooth as untapped water in a well, and nods, putting on the ghost of a smile. Mother beams at the acceptance.

Soon enough, Liesl gulps her food down and offers to wash the pots. There's something subtly anxious about her, as though she's been filled with a newly planted need for Mother's approval. Perhaps I'm imagining it; perhaps it actually is jealousy. I was no opponent, but there's a chance Renate could be a good daughter —competition.

Father chews absentmindedly, oblivious.

That night, I can't sleep. Renate is recovering surprisingly well, so she's been given a space in the attic with us. I can hear her breaths alongside those I'm used to.

It's dark. Weak slivers of moonlight seep through the shutters, but they are few and far between. My consciousness fades between waking and thin, fleeting dreams, until my ears are taken by an odd shuffling noise, loud against the breathing silence.

She has risen. A quiet shadow before my eyes, caught in the bleary dark. Unnoticed by the other two sleeping forms, she steps and dresses near-silently, witnessed only by the creeping whispers of sunrise. And me. She descends the ladder, which usually creaks, but now is rendered soundless by her feet. She's quick across the ground floor of the house—I soon hear the tiny creak of the front door.

Hurried but heavy, I rise too. I pass over the dark floor and wince at the noise the planks make as they bend. I climb down; the space is still and quiet, illuminated only by the crack of soft dawn light that falls from the open door. I go to it. The house does not stir. My boots lie near the frame, curled and cowering. I ignore them, hasty, and follow barefoot.

Outside, I see the movement of her dress and her quick shadow, curving round the wall of a distant building. With a swift glance about, checking for any eyes in the half-light, I set off after her.

The path has hardened since the day of my escape, rough to the touch of my bare feet. I thank Rhene; hard crumbs of dirt are easy to brush off—slick mud, less so. To be out of the home in the early hours of the morning—it's unbecoming, strange. It's something I want to keep to myself.

Curiosity and a keen eye pushes me forward through the little maze of Hanshen. The world lightens slowly; I can see her shadow even better now, shifting quietly behind her. She hasn't looked back at all, confident in her light stride towards the southern edge of the village.

When she gets to the village gate, I expect her to hesitate, faced with the field, and farther on, the wood, with its great wall of trees peeking over the horizon. The edge of the Path. If I glimpse the wood, It feels like I'm there again—the peace and the wonder and the shifting, chasing shadows. The sensation of watching witch-eyes, straying into the corners of my mind like sinister birdsong and shuffling spirits that are there and not, calling me to and away.

But Renate does not hesitate. My heart jumps strangely in my chest.

She starts over the field, the morning wind pushing strong behind her. There is no hiding now, behind corners, in shadows and walls; there is only the field, and if I follow her I make myself known. So I do, running towards her over the grasses. Before I'm even halfway there, she's turned, expectant. *Did she hear me just now, or has she always known?*

I approach. Here the wind is wild and free, rolling across undulating fields. The skirt of her dress dances. Her eyes are cool and dark. The scale on her necklace glints blue, exposed to the growing rays of sun. We stand across from each other, still, like statues caught in the freshness of the morning.

"What do you want?" Renate says, voice clear and strong. It jolts me. She has an accent, soft but firm, words rolling into one another. *What do I want?*

"To warn you," I begin. "The wood, it's strange—" I bite my words, ready to laugh at my hypocrisy.

It's dangerous, I want to say. But I didn't die there. *Do I really know anything? The peace I felt there was real, I'm sure of it, but were the shadows?*

It isn't clear; it's shifting in my memory, always shifting. I pray that Rhene is right, and then that he is not, over and over again. From behind Renate, the forest calls.

Yet I cannot go. I must be a good daughter. *A good woman.*

"It's dangerous." I say, "People don't come back."

I know she saw some conflict in me—her face is so focused with watching—but I will be stalwart from now on, righteous like the Speaker. Even though it's too late.

A smile, both wry and rueful, spreads across her face, of dry pity.

"Who would want to return to a place like this?" she asks. A coldness strikes my core.

"I have two choices." she hisses, "Escape across the sea, or escape through the forest. And one of your little boats will not protect me from that cursed sea."

Something sharp flickers in her twisted expression as she hisses the last sentence. Sparks of grief, and a crack in the mask that covers fear.

She turns towards the wood.

"Wait—" I breathe, surrendering to a long-moulded instinct. I grab at her wrist. She stops, as though tethered by a plaintive child.

"I will not stay here." she says, voice low.

But then tremors shake her words: "You heard. Even though they escaped the sea, my parents were taken by the water. And to

In the chaos of their noises I hear words—or fragments of words, at least. *Let, food, go, cold, out.* All in pieces, interspersed with rapid clucking. *Food, food, hungry, go, out, out.*

I'm going insane. The chickens are not supposed to talk. I try to stay away from the door to the pen, sticking to the furthest corners of the house, but I can still hear them, muffled and petulant.

My family returns. Mercifully, the chickens are asleep. I thank Rhene silently during our mealtime prayer. We eat. Mother complains that the stew is flavourless—it tastes as though I didn't put enough effort into it, she says. I can't help but wonder what she expected—it tastes the same as always to me.

Florian is asleep before I can ask him for a story, so I lie down and catch myself in restless, buzzing sleep.

The wood calls. I fight it.

The chickens wake me in the morning. *Run, food, out, grass, hungry hungry hungry.* I sigh, then go to feed them. They do seem as hungry as they were in my stupid imagining, but then again, they do always love to eat. Greedy things.

As days pass in a dull circle, it doesn't stop. They keep clucking for food, for warmth, at the things beyond their pen. And I *understand* them. *Why can I understand them? Has my mind left me? Did I drink saltwater without realising?*

My heart jolts with an awful shiver and the shadow of the Speaker looms over my mind. *Witches. They can do strange things.*

I stand in the pen attached to the back of our house. The chickens look normal. I stare. They cluck quietly.

"Hello?" I whisper to no one, eyes flicking around for people's shadows, or the sound of their breathing on the wind. *If anyone sees me...*

But it's alright; there's nothing. Then I look down, and the chickens have frozen, looking up at me in unison.

Oh no.

"Food?" I say quietly. One of their favourites, as I imagined. Yes, only imagined.

Then: *food, food, food, food.* I hear it around me, repeated back, an odd, clucking echo. *Oh Lord. Oh Rhene.*

I return to the house and sit at the table. Something is grinding against my bones and pulling my muscles taut. My lungs feel small, like pressure is slowly crushing them to dust. Frantic thoughts leap through my head. I know that I strayed from the Path. I'm trying to repay.

Witches cannot repay. They can only find Rhene after death, soaked in sea salt and cold.

Yet life continues normally. Mother finds the dust that I missed in the corners. I don't know how there's any left; I sweep all day. The soup is cold; I forgot to stoke the fire. My heart is shivering whenever any of my family are around me. Florian can see it—the leashed terror buried beneath my face. When he asks if I'm alright, I lie.

I'm bored, that's all. Just bored.

That night, I do not sleep. Not even a little. The chickens are awake, and the wood has tainted me.

Out, out, out, out, they say. *Let us out, let us out.* Their stupid, clucking voices echo in thick waves through my skull.

I toss and turn in the dark and feel an angry fire begin to eat my heart.

Father bolts out from the bedroom, pushing Liesl behind him. I see something other than his usual distance; he's looking at me, seeing me. It feels like the first time.

Florian descends the attic ladder frantically. When he sees me, his foot misses the next rung.

My skin simmers; I stand in my rage and pain, a beacon of weeping flame.

"Stay back!" I scream, clutching the panic set deep in my core, shivering in my burning bones. Whatever I am, it's dangerous. *They need to stay away.*

The table has caught fire; the floor is alight; the walls are burning. A sadness tinges my soul—the good daughter's fear for her family, sadness at her sin. But only for a moment. All of it is going up in flames and I do not mourn it. *Here is the raging girl, the spirit of fire. Here I am.*

I think they will run. Escape, do whatever they can to get out. When they do, Father remains, poised, as though faced with a beast. I understand. It's what I feel like. But I can't quench the flame. My rage is burning, my pain is seeping out in hot, unending waves. He runs forward. I'm a beacon. I do nothing but watch.

When he tackles me, fire licking at his forearms, there's a heavy shock, a snap inside me. In a flash, I no longer pour flame like water; a calmness seeps coldy into my veins. And then comes the panic again, subdued and weary—the realisation: I didn't choose it, but I am a witch. And here in Hanshen, each of my breaths may be my last.

Father does not let me go. Instead, he carries me out of our burning house. I hang exhausted in his arms, overtaken by heat. I am void of energy, one with the quiet darkness of the sky above.

A crowd hovers around our house in a hushed clamour,

watching it burn in the dark of the early morning. I crane my neck and look back, blurry eyed.

It's terrible. It's bright.

5

The Hold is dark and damp, rust-barred and kissed by mocking salt wind. I was locked in here an hour ago, and the sun hasn't risen.

I am waiting. At dawn, the Speaker said, I will feel the justice of Rhene, for what I am.

What am I?

I knew I was different, strange. But not a witch. Never a witch; unless the chickens, stupid as they were, were evil spirits, I haven't been fed evil by any. I can't do spells or wicked forest charms. *All I did was—*

Fire flickers across my memory. I throw my fist against the stone wall, summoning pain to quell it.

I sit in a curved, barrel-like structure, built of barnacled stone by our ancestors—a prison built into the cliff, overlooking the sea. Sinners must repent here, but I can't return from what I've done. I will be drowned at dawn.

There hasn't been a witch drowned since I was born.

I imagine the sea reclaiming me. The mercy of Rhene, felt only as he steals my breath and kills my body. Watery tendrils, pulling me down forever.

As my palm scrapes against the rough rock, I feel markings. Those who were here before me, waiting in the dark. Their pain, their waiting—it all floods into me, and I want to cry. I want to let loose the hot, fiery tears I kept inside me. I have so many more to give.

The house flickers again, unwanted in my mind. Fire, pouring from my hands.

I shiver. *How, Lord Rhene? How did I do that? Why have you cursed me?*

I wonder if it was for being who I am—a bad woman. The worst daughter. Unworthy to even be a wife.

Perhaps I should welcome my death.

As I was carried away, Mother did not speak. All she did was look in the other direction. Liesl was frozen, staring from the comfort of her arms.

And Florian—I've never seen him make a face like that. There should be spacing or punctuation between "Florian" and "I've". Agony, disbelief, pity: all mixed in a bubbling pool, shining through like blinding light.

I sigh. Exhaustion aches in my bones. I am a shell that nurtures a dying flame.

Die, they say. Let the water put you out.

A flicker. I open my eyes, scared of my own memory. But there it is: one flicker, then another, and another. I see a torch, a flame bobbing at the door.

A trembling whisper comes from the light.

"Kestra."

The pain sitting in my core flares, heavy and deep. I know that voice immediately, even marred by worry and sleeplessness. It's Florian. He shouldn't be here—to see me now will make my death worse for him later. Speaking with the dead is pointless—the only thing to gain is heartache.

"Why are you here?" I whisper back. "You saw. You saw it all."

"I did."

"Then why come to speak to a dead girl?" Angry tears well in the corners of my eyes.

"You aren't a witch." he murmurs, reaching through the bars, "I don't believe it."

I don't know what to say. He saw, but says this. I remember his bright-eyed terror; it was real enough.

Despite everything, though, I take his hand through the bars and hold on as though my life depends on it.

"When I saw you there, so upset, you just looked like someone who was hurt." he says. It's a lovely lie. I can imagine what I actually looked like: a terrible inferno, fiery-eyed and wrathful. A monster. *A witch.* But Florian is kind; he's always kind. Something inside me cracks. My tears start to fall—I'm melting into despair.

He grasps my hand harder; his eyes are wet, too.

"I don't know what's happening," he says, "But I know it isn't your fault."

His voice cracks, and he takes a breath, shaky but decisive.

"You don't deserve this. If Rhene wants you dead, he's wrong," He pulls his hand from mine and fumbles with something, face set in determined righteousness. Tears are running thick down his cheeks. "He's *wrong.*"

There's a grating click, and the Hold's door creaks open. My stomach drops. *He stole the key from the Speaker.* Limbs frozen with cold and shock, I let him drag me out and fold me into his arms.

The sea air is now full and harsh on my face; I'm no longer assailed by the creeping, mocking tendrils that air the Hold. I breathe deep and savour the life in my chest. I try to steady my fear —for Florian, for myself—and clear my mind. Panic bubbles as I try to change my vision of the future, of what could be. Seconds ago it was death—all I could imagine was the embrace of the water. Now it's all uncertain. All I know is that I cannot stay here.

The wood is calling. Always calling—even now, as I stare out at the dark ocean, searching for Rhene's signs in vain. *Perhaps my decision has always been made. Perhaps ever since that day in the wood, my path has been set.*

Florian is pulling me towards the shore path. "I can help you get away in a boat," He says, frantic.

I pull my hand from his grip.

"No. Don't risk any more for me. I wouldn't know how to handle one, anyway. We never did end up sailing together."

I wink one tearful eye and grin through the salt that stains my face. My chest is full to bursting. When I look into his tearful eyes, I can see he understands. The wood is where I'm going, and this is a goodbye. Even if he wanted to, he can't leave our family. They need him, and there would be no coming back.

I embrace him first, this time. I pull him close, with a mournful desperation.

"I hope you know that I loved all your stories, Florian." I whisper, voice cracking. The tears are flowing again.

"You were the best audience I could ask for," he says, trying to chuckle and release us both from some pain. He hugs me back, hard, as though he's holding on for his life. He hands me a pack from his back; I thank him and give him one last hug, the corners of my mouth trembling.

"My little sister." he croaks. He presses his salt-chapped lips to my forehead. We stand in that moment for as long as we can.

And then we part. I walk away from Florian and the shore. I pass the moonlit Lord's Chapel, its crumbling stone structures like bones silhouetted against the night. I am quiet, a shadow again, traversing the edge of Hanshen. I'm unseen and unseeing, stranger to all but the wood. It pulls me closer and closer.

I stand at the boundary.

It is dark; already I see the shadows, shifting and changing behind my back. I let myself be reminded of my fear, and then I kill it. Rhene has cast me from his Path, and I grieve it. But now the only path is south.

Dawn's first rays push me forward and the wood engulfs me. I don't look back. I can't.

II: SHROUDED SPARKS

6

THE WOOD RISES with the dawn.

Pack strapped securely to my back, I watch the shadows fade
and hiss as golden light patters through the trees and lands at my
feet. My boots are fast and knowing, treading the path I went once
before. The clear smell of the morning envelops me, devoid of salt
and filled with chirping birdsong.

Then I hear it again: the grey bird. Its haunting song echoes
amongst the branches, caught in the leaves. Despite my aching
chest, and the weight of tiredness and change that I drag behind,
there is a surface salve of peace around me, inexplicable and
welcome.

If I am branded a witch, is this not my place?

I travel for an hour or so, traversing the seeking roots and
green moss, finding the hand-hold hollows of the great trees and
feeling their solid bark. They ground me, taking me from a head
swirling with memories of Florian's face, and my family, faced
with the terror of fire.

Soon, though, I cannot go on. The chickens made sure I had no sleep, and there was certainly none to be had in the Hold. The whirlwind of the morning has taken all I have to give; I must rest. My unfocused stare finds a large tree, broad and tall. I find a kind dip in its roots, covered with moss, and sit, putting the pack Florian gave me on the ground beside me.

In it, there are blankets. Water from the well, in bottles. Food: dried fish and dusty biscuits. I say a silent thank you to Florian, then lie down to sleep.

Flame licks my dreams. There comes my rage, fierce and righteous. I dream of Hanshen burning; a cold village made warm. When I am conscious, I know my guilt; I know my sadness. But deep in my mind there is something different, raw and roiling. A child told they are wrong for who they are—for what they can do. In this world, I see only with eyes of bright, leaping flame, and everything burns. Everything.

A rustle. I rise with a jolt, remembering the fear of last time, of witches and spirits and bears. Then I take a breath. *I was alright then; it was nothing. Nothing but my own mind.*

Another rustle. Voices. My spine straightens, muscles growing taut. Last time, I did not conjure voices. And these don't sound like the repetitive cries of the chickens.

I put on my pack and crouch low, glancing around. The voices are getting closer, with heavy steps to match them, grumbling through forest grasses. My chest is tight. *Where do I go?*

Running on nothing but instinct, I look up. Thick branches

arch above me; the canopy contains an obscuring darkness. I'm sure of this much: they won't be coming from above.

So I begin to ascend, clumsy and breathless. Hands on bark, feet scrabbling at the rough surface of the tree, finding places to stand, to rise, to climb. I get a hold, up and up, until I reach the proper branches, and then it becomes easier; there's something to stand on, to grab, to pull me up again and again. By the time I look back down, I've climbed high—the forest floor is difficult to see, obscured by all the branching life around me. The leaves are everywhere up here, twisting on their branches; this place is an entire world away from the ground.

I see movement below. Three figures move towards where I once was, slow and careful. I squint, then my stomach drops. They wear fisherman's garb. *They're from Hanshen. Why are they here? Is this not past the edge of the Path?*

Perhaps they see me as too dangerous to live, even outside Rhene's jurisdiction. I could return, cloaked in deadly fire. If I can imagine it, they can too.

I watch them search, and wait, breathless, for them to look up, to see the shadow curled amongst the dark leaves. My heartbeat thrums in my ears. *If they find me, will I have to burn them? Can I even muster the strength?* I search for whatever anger made the inferno mere hours earlier, but I find nothing but fear. Painful, shaking fear—at the memory itself; at my family's eyes, bright and terrified, fearing only me. And still, I hang poised, straining, palm out, ready to push whatever heat I can find from my veins.

Nothing comes.

After while of crouching in the branches, I watch them leave. They move like scared animals, jerky and watchful. *To risk their lives and brave the edge of the Path... All to find me.* I have become

If they'd found a place like this, alive and warm, wouldn't they have returned to tell us?

I slow my pace and reach out to a door frame, feeling the old wood's cracks and hollows. A strange tale sits beneath the surface of this whole place, I know it. I peek inside the home. It is small. Foliage pushes through the plank floor and a sunbeam falls in from above, through a tear in the latticework of the roof. There's a bedframe, like the one my parents have, and what looks like a crib. Dust dances slowly in the light's thin gold. I'm frozen in strange, melancholy wonder.

Who lived here?

Was this place a witch-town when it was alive, woven with evil magic? My heart, ever-buried in the warmth of my imaginings, says no. It must have been a lovely place, for a while. Then something in the wood must have got to it—though of course, I cannot be sure.

Here, having left the Path, I know punishment is coming—perhaps it did for these people. I've just been lucky so far. It's strange to be in such a peaceful place whilst this deep dread swirls beneath the surface of my mind.

With a heavy heart, I leave the village behind, pressing on towards what I think is south. After having been in the wood so long, it all begins to look the same: peaceful, but with an unnerving repetitiveness that worries me. I'm not a navigator. Women aren't taught to navigate—it's a skill only needed on the sea.

Vines curl above and moss amasses beneath my boots; trees stand green and tall and never end. The grey bird sings. I think it's following me. I see flickers of it up in the trees, sometimes, but I don't need to; I know when it's there by what it sounds like—like nothing else I've ever heard, haunting and sweet and clear.

Days pass. *Are these moments the beginnings of my new life, or the last before I die?*

I don't know. The grey bird stops singing at points, and I find myself drawn to where I last heard it, following without realising.

I refilled my bottles at the stream by the ruined village, but my food is running out. There are berries abound, and nuts, which I collect as best I can, but I can't be sure which ones are poisonous, caught in a witch-curse. That is the true danger of this forest: all appears bountiful and safe, yet beneath it all lies something I don't understand.

So I conserve food. I sleep. I dream of fire. I wake, disquieted. I drink. I follow the bird. It all repeats, again and again. I am trekking, weary, through the wood, and it looks the same as it always has.

Then, one morning, I find the bodies of the fishermen. They're like rocks on the forest floor, heaped and jagged. Vines entangle them. Here, silence suffocates the air and a deep dread threatens to knock me from my feet.

A hand. A leg. A pale, pale face. I've seen a handful of drowned bodies, lost for breath. These ones certainly have none left. The air is gone from them, strangled out; I can see it in their skin, and in the tight vines that wrap their necks.

The unease that has been simmering comes to a boil. Bile rises in my throat and a shivering panic threatens to take me... I keep it down. *I must be calm; I must be wary. I will not meet their fate.*

My brain flurries with questions: *Did witches do this? Or is the wood itself alive? If so, why was I not strangled in my sleep?* My blood suddenly runs cold—perhaps I really am one of the witches, now, immune to the wiles of the wood.

Complete the death rites, my mind says. *They are from Hanshen. Rhene must see them through.*

But there is no sea here, past the bounds of the Path, and no Rhene. I don't want to come near the bodies; I don't want to touch the vines. They radiate the danger of clever killing—they're so thin, yet somehow stronger than sea-worn fishermen.

The grey bird is not singing, but my journey resumes, farther and farther in towards where I last heard it. I leave the bodies with an eerie tingling on the back of my neck.

Soon, I find another stream—a blessing, if I wasn't now deathly afraid of this wood's motives. Starting at every movement and creature, I make my way through the undergrowth. I bind my mind and make it unwandering, focused only on the space ahead.

When I curl up in another hollow, I pick a tree that's vineless, and try not to imagine the roots moving and seeking for my body's air. The cut on my arm aches, though I cleaned it as best I could at the stream.

I fall asleep with a trembling heart and an arm that throbs harshly to its stuttering beat.

7

I START awake and smack my head against the tree trunk with a yelp.

A dark morning is breaking. The wind whistles and the wood undulates with weak light. I watch the moss, ruffled by a shadowed breeze. For a few minutes, there is peace. I have woken, ruffled, for nothing.

No going back now. I start to pack up my things, folding my blankets. I eat the last of my food: half of a crumbling biscuit. And then I hear it.

Something is coming; I'm not imagining it this time. I hear it trudging towards where I am. Back pressed flat against the tree, I hold my breath. My heartbeat rattles loudly and I hope it's only me that can hear the sound of it. But the trudging moves closer. I glance around to my things, considering taking them up and running.

A shadow approaches, hulking, snuffling.

Frozen, I stare: thick fur, brown and coarse; a dark snout; flashing eyes. Claws that scrape the forest floor with every step. Static floods everything I am; I buzz with cold fear. *This is a bear. Is* this a bear?

The air between us is cold and prickling. The Speaker never told us how to deal with bears—he just warned us that they lay beyond the bounds of the Path: our punishment.

How do you approach one? Do you run? Do you roar? Do you try to make it calm?

Irritation stains its beady eyes. I remember the chickens. I remember their voices. *Can I...?*

"Hello," I say, voice trembling. "I mean no harm... I..."

It advances, slowly. A sickness flows through me and sticks in my stomach.

"Do you understand?" I whisper frantically. My feet are retreating on their own, but my back soon hits the tree. The bear's muscles tense beneath the fur; its eyes throb with anger as they stare down at me. I catch a fragment of something intelligible, interspersed with a low, guttural rumbling.

Our land, it says. *Our Duskwood.*

I am frozen. It's a huge beast, tall on all fours, but when it rears onto its hind legs I stifle a scream.

Fire. I reach for it without thinking. I need it: my fire. *Where is it?* My palms are hot, but only with sweat. Blood runs fast to my head, swirling and pumping, and I focus, I strain, I—

The bear swings with a gigantic claw and I duck, thrown from everything I was attempting.

Then I live only in snatchings of seconds.

It growls and swings again; I dodge, nerves tingling, and

stumble backwards, grabbing a high branch. I pull myself up with an unexpected strength, breathless, crouch on the wood and stare at its upturned eyes, desperate to feel its anger, take some for myself, as fuel. I focus. *Fire. Hanshen, burning. Palms, hot, pouring fire—*

The branch shudders violently. A clawed paw bashes again and suddenly my feet find nothing—I fall backward and air rips cruelly past. I hit the ground—slamming pain cracks through my back and all breath is torn from my lungs. From the ground, the bear looks even bigger, a heaving goliath, paw ready to slam—

I roll, but the claws catch my injured arm and *then* I find a form of fire, in the shape of pain burning deep through my screaming body. *Useless.*

It pulls back for another swipe and I scramble up, running and falling through the undergrowth, caught amongst the roots and the moss; birds startle, little creatures run and burrow, my feet thump. I hear it coming; I'm ready to feel its claw rip through my back, ready for the blood, *oh Rhene, make me ready—*

Something crashes from behind, but I don't feel any pain.

A furious howl shakes the wood. Then there's another noise: a fierce growl in return. I turn, shaking, and see another bear rearing up between us, light furred and much smaller.

It's half the size of the giant that's been chasing me, but it stands strong, as though in a conscious stance. Enraged, the giant flies at it, but it ducks away and swipes once with its claws, narrowly missing the giant's eye.

Ripping my own eyes from the tussle, I scramble up the closest tree, skinning my palms painfully against harsh bark. A rumble sounds from below, shaking the entire wood, and in a he's probably a forest spirit, or some other strange thing that the Speaker didn't mention. I should be scared of him, whatever he is, but he just seems like a normal boy—he even looks about my age, if not a little short.

"I don't think so," he replies. "I'm a druid. We just live here."

"There are more of you?"

"South of here. The bears like to roam around this part of Duskwood, so we give them space."

Duskwood. The bear said it too. Is that the wood's name?

We never named it, as far as I know—it never needed naming. There was only Hanshen, and the edge of the Path—and that didn't matter in daily life. It was only something to be avoided.

"I can take you there," he offers. "It's a safer place—you look like someone who might need one."

A chill of rejection runs through me. *I don't need help.* I'm not the one who's different here; it's this witch-boy and his odd magic.

Rationality soon comes through, though—he'll know what is safe to eat, and I've run out of safe food. *And* he took down a bear twice his size.

He seems nice, even quite normal, ignoring the fact that he can turn into a bear. *The boy and his father from our village, the ones that never came back. Did they make it to the place he is offering to lead me to?*

Everything in my body tingles with uncertainty. I hear the Speaker in my head, warning of the evils of witches and the wiles of forest spirits. But he never went into the wood. *The Duskwood.*

He didn't even know its name, I think indignantly. *How did he know anything at all, really?*

Besides, my only choice is to follow this boy or die to the next bear that comes along. And aside from that, I'm curious.

57

Something is whispering from within—the lover of stories, the desirer of adventures inside me. My curious heart may be caged, but I can't stop it from singing at me.

I sigh. *I suppose the decision was made from the start.* I straighten up; a pang shoots through my arm.

"Fine." I say coolly, "I wouldn't mind seeing it."

Whatever happiness he would have had at my acceptance is dampened by his concern at the sight of my arm. I was clutching it before, but now it is bare; blood is dripping from the wound, made fresh again by sharp bear claws.

"Can I help?" he asks, and though he's much shorter than me, in that moment, I see my brother in him. It's strange—I shouldn't hear the tone of anyone I know in a witch-boy. They're different from us. Wicked and wrong, unknown to Rhene.

I'm unknown to Rhene, now, I remind myself. *And the Speaker didn't actually meet anyone from beyond the Path.*

I let him clean my arm and bandage it with a soft cloth that he produces from his woven bag. We sit quietly on the forest floor, and though bears apparently roam this area, I feel safer than before. The throbbing soon lessens; relief floods through me. I grew used to feeling a little pain at every movement—perhaps that can change again, and I can be free of it.

When he's finished, I ask: "Who am I thanking for this help?"

"Conrad." he says simply, picking himself up and glancing around. He stares at the sunlight through the canopy and sniffs as though some invisible scent is carrying through the trees. "Yours?"

"Kestra."

I reveal my name to him without thinking—though I omit my family name; it is mine no more. I suppose I'm just Kestra now, a wanderer in the wood.

too many people, but I see some walking as we reach the great tree. One is tall, dark skinned and short haired, another is pale and slight; both wear similar robes in deep greens and browns. There's a calmness to them.

This place is so hushed. I feel the presence of something sacred.

Then I see her in the distance.

Renate, unmistakably. Dark-eyed, bronze skinned, with a stillness in her gaze that slides off me like water. She stands outside the houses, leaning against a wall, enrobed in the deep greens of this place. Her face shines out at me, caught in a thinned sunbeam.

My head turns toward her without meaning to, magnetised by an inexplicable force. *She survived.*

I cannot speak to her now, though; Engelberta pulls me ahead around the great tree, to the southern path. Conrad has drifted away—it's just us two now, heading towards a great stone building.

It reminds me of the Chapel, but it's different in the ways that are important: though ancient, it seems loved rather than dilapidated—and, as all things seem to be here, one with the wood.

Moss creeps up its sturdy walls; ivy reaches down from the top of its tower. The right of it extends out, shorter in height but still tall; windows of coloured glass peer from its walls. At the building's curved eastern wall, the roof opens, and a tree's broad branches stretch up over its edges.

"This is our church," Engelberta says in her creaking, comforting voice. "The Church of our Oakfather, who helps us druids protect this wood."

"Who?"

She chuckles. "There is much to explain."

We enter the church. There are stairs leading up to the next floors of the tower, but she instead leads me right, through a stone archway.

Pews line each side of the room. Vines and flowers hang from the ceiling, and sunlight streams in ribbons from the windows. Ahead is the tree I saw, broad-branching and tall, its trunk comfortably nestled in a roofless, walled semicircle of stone. Unlit lanterns hang from its branches. The stone floor fades to grass and moss as the room continues to its curving end.

At the foot of the tree, Engelberta sits. When she gestures in front of her, I go to the soft moss and sit too, still wondering at the space around me. It's beautiful, all of it. And so peaceful—like seeing Duskwood again for the first time.

"Nature is beautiful, isn't it, Kestra?" Engleberta says, as though reading my mind. Her green eyes study me and her voice draws my focus back to her. She plucks a fallen leaf from the ground beside us and holds it delicately between two fingers.

"It is fragile, too. Precious."

I can see the signs of decay on the leaf, long disconnected from its life source—its greenness is fading.

"We can protect it," she continues. "And in turn, it protects us."

My eyes do not leave the leaf; something strange is happening. A fresh green hue creeps up its stem from her fingers. Imperfections from its time on the ground—tears and rips and all else—are fixed, made whole. It's beautiful—a tide of life, unstoppable from her hand. I can't look away.

"Life can come from us, as well as this wood." she says, raising her other hand.

"The wind," she whispers. I feel a breeze slip through this place; the tree sways above.

"The water," A ball forms slowly above her hand, like a gigantic floating jewel, undulating in the light. It's made of water, clear and cool. She lets it fall to the grass.

"The earth." Her hand brushes the grass, and it grows, like months and years are passing, curling up and up. She raises her hand up and I watch the tree sway above. A bud sprouts on one of its low branches.

Witch, my mind says.

But my heart knows better.

This feels right. This connection, I've always felt it. I remember my first venture in the Duskwood. The peace. The wholeness. *What harm can it be to create life?*

And yet, there's something missing. Fire flashes across my memory. I don't want it, but it was there, real enough for them to want me dead. I wouldn't be here otherwise.

"What about fire?" I say.

This time, her silence is not warm. Worry creeps behind her eyes, and momentarily, her face becomes rigid. Then, with a sigh, she speaks.

"I understand your curiosity, child. But to create fire with the power that the Oakfather has given us is dangerous—a terrible sin."

A sick, ugly coldness seeps into my stomach. I do my best to mask whatever expression I may have made, and nod slowly.

"We give life." she continues. "And we protect this wood. Fire and smoke, untamed, know only destruction. And those who destroy must in turn be cleansed, for the good of all who live."

A shiver jitters through me. As she speaks, I notice the leaf in her hand returning to its previous state. Life seeps from it like blood.

"Where I came from, Kestra—" She pauses to cough. When she looks up, her brow is furrowed deeply. "Death is the only thing that follows fire, whether fast or slow. I am old, compared to you. I have seen what fire does in its masses, untamed in human hands. I have—" She pauses again, and there's an even deeper heaviness to her face. "I have lost people that I love."

I don't know what to say. Something cold is eating at my insides.

She returns to her point: "Fire is not used the way we use the other elements. The Oakfather does not wish for it."

She almost spits the last sentence—it's strange to see someone so calm become so ruffled. My question was a stone, thrown hard at a still lake.

The hollow, sick feeling will not leave me. The leaf in her hand is black. I try not to stare, but when it crumbles in her clenched grasp I cannot help but flinch.

She notices, then looks back at me.

"I apologise. These things matter dearly to me. Soon enough you will understand. In fact, I sense you may already be one of us."

A chill strikes my spine again. *Does she know?* My body is cold, but my mind is hot with fire; it won't leave. I can feel it, caught deep in my blood. *A sin here as it was there.*

As we rise, she shows no further sign of anger. I take a breath. *She doesn't know. She can't know.* I remember the grey bird, how it followed me at first, then led me through the wood... But I never saw it *in* Hanshen; I never saw *her* in Hanshen. She has seen no fire. I repeat it over and over in my mind as we walk out.

With each turn of the thought it becomes stronger. It soothes me.

Conrad is waiting outside. He looks to Engelberta, who nods minutely.

"I can show you where we sleep." he says.

They all assume I'm staying. It's irritating, but they're right. *Where else would I go? Back to the bears, to get torn to shreds?*

Despite the quiet fear simmering beneath my skin, watching Engelberta's magic made my heart sing.

I *want* to stay, despite the secret sin shivering inside me.

So I follow Conrad up the path and leave Engelberta behind. The weight of her eyes soon falls from my back and I can breathe again; the peace returns. Conrad may be a strange boy, able to turn into a bear, but the atmosphere around him is unfailingly warm. He bows to the few people we pass—a strange greeting in my eyes, but I'm in Hanshen no longer, so I follow his example.

They all look at me kindly. I must look awful, in my muddy, ripped dress, worn for days upon days. Tiredness pulls at my edges, and despite the cleaning, my wound still aches. The thought of somewhere to sleep sounds wonderful.

We come to the cluster of buildings I saw Renate around before. Up close, the structures are even more beautiful. I understand a little more now, after seeing Engelberta work with the elements—the people here converse with nature; I see it in everything. The vines wrap these buildings tightly, holding up their stone. Flowers bloom on foreign surfaces, filling every inch with life.

Renate is nowhere to be seen.

Conrad shows me into the middle building. It's only one storey; snug passages lead comfortably into similar rooms. Each one contains a few woven hammocks, alongside simple wooden furniture and other trinkets. I notice a few candles, as well. My mind goes running, working to figure out exactly how non-magical fire is treated. I've seen candles and lanterns, so a little must be allowed. But I don't feel safe asking about fire anymore, so instead I ask Conrad about the wooden things.

"We use only as much as we need," he replies. "And we replant the trees in full."

By this time, we've arrived in the end room.

"This is where I sleep right now," he explains, "there's a spare hammock."

I scour the room. It's bare but cosy—I can't complain. Three hammocks. Small windows. When Conrad leaves, I feel my energy winding down; the sight of a place to sleep is already sapping it away.

I fall asleep with the knowledge that this place will be safe—if I'm careful. As long as I'm careful, everything will be fine.

9

THE FIRST THING I see when I wake up is Renate. I start and sit up in my hammock, almost falling out. She's sitting right in front of me, on a wooden dressing table.

"You made it." she says matter-of-factly. "I knew you wanted to get out."

Anyone else would be smirking, but her expression remains as unreadable as a still pool. I don't quite know what to say; I'm still caught in the clouds of sleep. Instead, I give her a tentative smile, brain working to find a response. She speaks before I can think of anything.

"Anyway, don't expect to see me around here for long."

What is that supposed to mean?

But she doesn't elaborate further.

A snuffle and a yawn sounds behind and I see Conrad's fluffy head pop up from a nearby hammock.

"Morning..." he mutters. He rubs his eyes, rolls out of his hammock and begins to shuffle towards us. "Kestra, this is—"

"We've met." Renate says. She turns to me. "So, how'd you end up leaving?"

I freeze. Fire flickers across my memory.

Conrad plops down on the floor and we find ourselves huddled in a lopsided circle. The air between us is hushed, and I can see the expectant tension in their posture. With their eyes fixed on me, I try to think of something to say—something that doesn't involve fire. But all there is is the night I left. I can see only the Hold and the raging fire and my burning palms and their faces, bright with fear...

"I let the chickens out."

They stare incredulously. Conrad's face is slack with bewilderment. A bemused smile pulls at Renate's mouth.

At the sight of her amusement, an unexpected spark of joy wells up inside me. My fear melts away—whatever I've started here, I want to continue.

"What?" I exclaim. "Once they realised I understood them, they kept me up all night."

Conrad laughs. "I see. Engelberta could tell you had felt the presence of the Oakfather."

As I watch him chuckle openly, I feel a little safer in speaking. *Perhaps I can ask him questions that I'd be too afraid to ask Engelberta.*

"You people keep mentioning the Oakfather—who is he?"

"Our god. The god of Duskwood and the natural world, whose laws we druids live by."

In my mind, I cannot help but hear the croaking drone of the Speaker: our Father, Lord Rhene, who rules us mercifully, *and on and on and on...* But it's not the same. This Oakfather must be fairer. He must be wiser. His must be the power of Engelberta,

70

with the sweet winds in her hands and her undulating jewel of water. It looked natural; it looked *right*.

And yet it's all tainted by fear. A blackened leaf, crumbling in her hand.

"Engelberta," I ask tentatively. "Where did she come from? She said..."

Conrad furrows his brow, thoughtful.

"She told me, once, when I was very young..."

After a beat, I see the light of the memory in his eyes. "A place to the south of the Spires—Brennof."

Florian's tales flood back to my mind in a rushing river of colour. Brennof: the great trading city. The lilt of Florian's voice in his imitation of a particularly eccentric trader—I had no way to tell then if it was accurate or just Florian's colourful addition, but now I see it must have been a true representation; I heard it beneath her voice.

"When you were young?" Renate asks, "What, were you born here or something? I didn't think any of us were."

"She took me in as a baby, when there was no one else that cared." Conrad replies. With a sigh, he picks himself up from the floor and gives his knees a dusting.

"I return her care in kind. We all should—she does a lot for us. And her health has been worsening for as long as I can remember."

After another pause, he rejuvenates himself, strides to the door and calls back to us: "Come on out, then! Don't you want to learn to do more than just speak to chickens?"

We start with the elements.

Morning light flits through the short trees of the grove. Engelberta stands rooted amongst them, her tall silhouette set firm against pale yellow light. Next to her stands the man I saw before, short haired and dark eyed: Otto, his name is.

Renate stands beside me, and Conrad too. The feel of new woven cloth against my skin is strange; I'm someone else now.

I get the impression that I'm the newest. There are a handful of us here, ready to learn, but I don't know them—though they seem about my age. Shyly, they introduce themselves to me: Ari, Leot and Ilse. Ari is almost as short as Conrad, heavily freckled with short ginger hair that sticks up from their head like ruffled grass. Leot is tall, and has similar features to Renate, though his hair is slightly shorter and his eyes are a light blue. Ilse's hair falls in long, curling tresses, almost white in its blondeness, though her skin is as dark as Otto's.

None of them speak much; nervousness is pouring from all of us in waves. We're all just kids, and from what Renate said, I can assume that this place is fairly new to us all.

I wonder how they ended up here.

We are split off into two groups. Engelberta comes to us first —Renate, Conrad and I. At the sight of her looking at me, a nervous tension pulls at my body.

"Conrad," she intones warmly, "I'm sure you can handle this. Of course, I recommend beginning with earth."

Conrad nods.

When she leaves, we begin. Conrad places his hands on the ground, and signals for us to do the same.

"Renate, I know you've done this before, but work with me." he says. He looks me in the eyes. "Take a deep breath and feel the earth beneath your hands. It has a heartbeat, like you and me."

This is stupid, my mind says. Still, I close my eyes and take a breath. *The way I first felt in Duskwood was real. I can find it again.*

The grass is soft, damp with beads of morning dew. I search farther beneath it, feeling for the dark spirals of the earth with both hands. *A beat.* Then another. Rumbling, rolling, singing through my fingers. It spreads through me like the fire, but slower and more rhythmically. Every particle vibrates individually, and I feel it clearly—I feel it all.

The heartbeat of the earth.

When I open my eyes, the grass around my hands has grown taller. Conrad claps his hands encouragingly. "Well done!"

When I look to his patch of grass, it is not only larger, but has beautiful flowers twisting amongst the elongated blades.

I stare, transfixed and eager. And this becomes my world.

Through many rolling green dawns, I learn the fresh scent of the grove at morning and become accustomed to the creaking sound of Engelberta's voice, dipping in and out of our two groups. Renate's silence folds itself into my sense of normality; Conrad's encouragement brings me small sparks of joy despite its frequency. Daily, I enjoy the warm, earthy flavour of Otto's delicious broths, in the smoothness of carefully carved wooden bowls. The Oakfather becomes less of a story and more of a reality; now I can make grass grow faster and weave tree branches like thread. I ask Conrad about other elements, and about shapechanging like he and Engelberta do.

"In time," he says. "When she says you're ready, you will be."

When Summer arrives and we move on from earth, Renate is

more brilliant than ever—that's the only way my struggling heart can describe her. In working with earth, she was my equal—but in mastery of water, she is something else.

The first day of learning the new element, we all go west, to the hot spring. It runs south, clear and teeming with life. It's so unlike the sea. The longer I stare, the more it seems as though there's liquid sunlight in it.

We start from here, Engelberta says, as creating water from the moisture in the air is difficult. But not for Renate. Though the still pool of her face becomes pinched with the ripples of fear at the sight of a body of water—I remember her family's bloated, gold-adorned corpses—she masters it and shows that her hands were made to weave what is hidden in not only the spring or sea, but the air. Delicate, jewelled streams of water are her threads to weave, sparkling with undiscovered light. Engelberta stands proud, filled with serene praise. Conrad is excited, as always.

He's with us like our shadow.

At first, his constant presence confused me a little, but I think he might have been lonely before we came here—there were others, but none even close to being as young as us. We're becoming a trio—it's nice. Like having a family that I've chosen to spend time with.

Unlike Renate, water is much harder for me to control. Earth is steady, easy to keep hold of, though hard to shift, but water is impossible, slippery as the stupid fish I used to have to gut. Despite my wonder at Renate's incredible displays, whenever we're supposed to work on it, my stomach drops nauseatingly. Every drop of water slips and slides from my grasp as though it wants to get away—once I think I even saw Renate stifle a laugh as I splashed myself in the face.

. . .

At night, in my lonely hammock, I listen to Conrad's snoring and Renate's invisible breaths.

I let myself remember my home—the cadence of my siblings' own drowsy breathing; the whispered stories of Florian. Conrad constantly reminds me of him—in time away from learning about the Oakfather's gifts, he tells me about everything.

He speaks with reverence about the founder of this sanctuary of druids, Roth Duskwood, who seldom visits. He's neither human nor animal, but the virtues of both are within him, Conrad says. He has a voice like wind in the mountains, and he's searching for things of legend. Conrad isn't quite sure what those things are, but he's sure they're important.

Roth. I wonder if I'll ever meet him.

Other snippets of Conrad's ramblings contain information about the different plants and animals of Duskwood, and the stories and songs of the trees. They sway in the air and talk, he says. I don't think I can hear them that well yet—it's just the occasional animal. A clipped bird call becomes a word; snuffling squirrels flee with a frantically whispered phrase.

Otto can tell that I hear them. He smells like his warm, well-spiced cooking, and he's very tall, like a broad tree. He can speak to animals like they're his old friends; often birds will swarm around him like friendly bees, singing sweetly. When he speaks back it sounds like them: a soft and ancient song, conveying something I simply cannot understand.

He can speak to plants, too. Sometimes I see him place his hand on the central tree's bark (they're Oak trees, Conrad said, gifts from the Oakfather). After Otto makes contact with the bark, I don't know if I'm imagining the rumbling I hear—like the roots are twisting in the ground, jumping to speak with him.

"How do you do that?" I say, the third or fourth time I see him do it.

He jumps. It's sunset, quiet. The lanterns glow from the great Oak's branches. Gold and orange stream thinly down from the canopy, but everything is shadowed. It's not scary shadow, though. That's another thing I've learned during my time here: to be at peace with the dusk.

"I become very still," he replies, "and I wait."

I walk over and stand beside him, in the bright shadow of the tree's reaching branches. I place my hand on the bark, enjoying the intricate texture. He places his hand next to mine.

"If you want to learn, I'll teach you."

So I learn. There are so many dawns, so many dusks. Hanshen haunts my dreams less and less, though it still appears when I least expect it: the fire, their bright terror. I'm beginning to feel that it will never fully leave me be.

In our learning of the elements, air comes next, alongside the advent of Autumn. It's difficult to tame, Engelberta says, and can be very dangerous, but it's available in abundance. My brain hears echoes of fire in her words—untamed, untamable—and cries out against it. *I cannot afford to be that person, here or anywhere.*

To harness that which moves, she says, first become aware of it.

Though fear shook my insides at first, when I harness the wind, there is only joy in my heart. Air currents race wonderfully across my skin without much effort at all.

Engelberta is right: after stillness comes movement. First, I sit quietly—then I am able to will breezes through the low trees of the grove, turned into a sea of reds and oranges by the season. Then the air moves to the rhythm of my own dancing; we work together, and sometimes I feel my very body lifted by the strength of it. Despite that, it remains wild and difficult—any change can send it spiralling—but with each dawn I react quicker, tracing the patterns in its dance by the flowing of fallen leaves and the sensation of power in its invisible wings.

These days, whenever we practise, there's a crack in my focus. Each breeze is punctuated by a glance across the auburn treescape at Renate. It doesn't achieve anything—her face is unreadable, as always. Even when it shifts slightly, I don't know what it means. But I can't help it; questions run through my mind as though propelled by the wind in my hands. *Is she watching? What does she think?*

I would ask, but I fear she would just be silent.

Now that I've learnt to shape the wind, my dreams are rife with flame. I cannot sleep.

My barefoot steps pad lightly across the plank floor. I go east, traipsing into the wild forest behind our huts. It is dark and quite cold. The lanterns hang in the trees, providing little light and warmth in the distance. Soon they are gone. I wish I could stay bathed in those lights, asleep and unafraid. *But this has to stop.*

My ears prick for the sound of footsteps that aren't mine, and my eyes flit around constantly for the sight of the grey bird. *Engelberta cannot see this.*

Mercifully, there is no rooted silhouette, no breath like

creaking bark, no haunting birdsong. Enveloping me is only the noise of the wood, and the sound of my own blood, beating with fear of bears and memories of chaos out of the bounds of my new home: The Sanctuary of Druids. The Church of the Oakfather.

The Oakfather. Is he watching? Is that how he works?

I hope not.

After a while of stumbling through the dark, I find a glade. It is marked by a pool of moonlight; the canopy opens above and lets me breathe the sky. At its edge I see a great tree—*an Oak?*—covered in moss.

I hear no birdsong. I see no silhouettes.

I am still. Against the cold, blue night I imagine flame, red and biting. Feel the movement of everything but yourself, she said. If you know it, you can harness it.

But I make the fire, I think. It came from inside my body, out of nothing.

No matter. Still everything, and it will reveal itself.

A minute passes. Then another.

Nothing comes. All my palms feel is cool sweat. No heat. *Nothing.*

I can't do this anymore.

They have to come out.

The flames can't stay in my head, holding my dreams ransom in their white-hot grip. My heart begins to thud. I let the thoughts come in, all fire and destruction. *I'll lure them in. I'll cage them. I'll cut them out like rot.*

I know this destruction isn't what I am anymore; I've felt the wind, and the water, and the earth—I'm better now, not a destroyer. I ache to take the fire and crush it until only ash is left. My limbs strain with overflowing rage; I can feel it twist and claw over muscle, stretching against bone and sinew. I tense and draw my clenched fist back, ready to punch whatever I can find; *something, anything—*

A light, and a sizzling crack. My palm is hot; my fist is burning. The tree in front of me has been branded, bark seared and glowing in the shape of my fist. Trembling, I lower my fist to my face.

It glows. When I unfurl my hand: a flame, flickering at the tip of my finger. Like a candle, but waning more and more as my horror takes over.

I want to be sick. I thought I could let it all out at once and be rid of it, just like that. I'd never have to worry about it again. But there it still lies, flickering indifferently.

I did let it out before, but I didn't have any idea of what was going on then. *This time was supposed to be different.*

In my mind, the house flashes and flickers with my family's faces. The fire still bubbles angrily inside me, and I can't control it.

Grief folds over me like a heavy blanket and the flame on my finger dies before my eyes.

I'm too scared of myself not to run back to my hammock, curl up, and pretend it all never happened.

Tomorrow, Oakfather, please make me forget.

10

FOR THE REST of that night, I do not dream of fire. When I wake, unshaken, a quiet, unexpected joy leaps in my chest. *Perhaps, then... Last night... It worked a little?*

I let *something* out.

As we prepare for the day, Renate is staring at me. A chill of fear begins to creep up my spine. *Did she see me leave? No. They were both asleep.* When she comes up later to tell me I have some mushroom in my teeth, I let out an internal sigh of relief, though it's strange of her to speak about something so trivial.

My thoughts wander to other things. Today I feel freer. A load has been lifted from my back. I am stiller when searching for the wind, and more careful when controlling it.

I'm working under the kind eye of Otto when a grey bird swoops from above. Engelberta transforms right behind me and speaks:

"Well done, Kestra. You're making wonderful progress." The creak of her voice jolts up my spine, but I let myself take a breath

Paths, but seeing Otto's warmth quenched makes my heart sink like a stone.

"It's alright," he replies, taking a breath. "It's what the Oakfather wills. He is part of the Duskwood now."

I nod somberly, struggling against the sudden, drowning sadness that surrounds us.

"You understand that, don't you? Sometimes, people must die for the wood to live."

Otto's eyes are bright, but I am silent. I don't quite understand what he means. To try and distract myself, I look over to where Renate was.

She's gone—she must've left while we were talking.

When dusk begins to fall, Otto returns to the sanctuary. I stay out longer, balancing everything I've learned. *Otto's father is part of Duskwood now. Renate can sit like she's a stone, or a tree, at one with the wood. It looks effortless.*

That's it. Perhaps I'm trying too hard.

I sit there, close my eyes and breathe. *Just breathe.* Each element swirls and settles around me in an unreadable dance. The light breeze, the earth at my feet, the running stream, all music, playing at my gentle fingertips. I am aware of them all. *There is me; there is them, but in some places we blur—when I call the wind and become light; when my heartbeat and the earth's are one. Yes. It makes sense. I understand.*

Something lands on my shoulder—heavier than wind, though it doesn't seem to knock me out of this oneness. Part of me, then. Part of the wood.

It has breath, like me. And a heart. I can feel it.

I open my eyes.

It's a bird. Large, sleek, brown-feathered. Its eye is bright with understanding, a shining gold. My brain searches for Conrad's drawings. *What type of bird is this? What is its name? What is its story?* The pages flicker in my mind; the drawings move like ghosts and gain fleeting colour that they never had.

This is an eagle.

The moment I realise, it takes off again from my shoulder. Nevertheless, it came to me as though I was part of the forest. Bubbling elation rises in my chest. *Perhaps I will be ready for the ceremony after all.*

It's late as I traipse back to the grove, thankful for the bowl of hot broth Otto saved for me. We don't speak, but the smiles we exchange signify an understanding. *He did it, so I can too.*

The lanterns almost seem to float in the great Oaks above me. I head to the huts, full and ready to sleep. Our room is dark. At his end of it, Conrad's snoring overpowers the silence of the space. But something is missing—some*one*.

Renate isn't here. I quell the shivering panic that threatens to rear its head. She can take care of herself, I know that. But it's dark now—*where could she possibly go?*

Creeping from the back of my mind comes her stare from the morning after I went to the glade. I sigh. *Well, it can't hurt to check.*

Renate sits in a pool of moonlight, at the centre of the sea of grass. I am quiet, but she knows I'm there. She always does.

"If I'd known there was a place like this, I would've come sooner." she says, voice softer than usual in the cool night air.

I'm silent. My thoughts are buzzing, but the sight of her turned towards me in the moonlight stops any words from leaving my mouth.

"What?" she says, flashing her ghost of a smile. "Angry that I found it, too? You shouldn't leave so loudly in the middle of the night."

I glance past her at the tree, heart pounding. The charred scar I left on its trunk isn't too bad, not in this half-light. She wouldn't notice it unless she looked closely.

She's staring at me, expectant. I unruffle myself, and step forward into the moonlight. I take a breath and gaze up, drinking in our little patch of sky. I never seem to see it in the sanctuary.

"You could have just asked," I say, trying not to laugh at the absurdity of it.

She smiles wryly. "Well, no one was supposed to know. Let's keep it a secret."

Even though I found this place, it feels like hers right now, draped in cool blues and drenched in cold moonlight.

I join her in the sea of grass, illuminated in the light of the moon. We stare up at it together, the moon alone in a starlit sky. The space is thin between us. I stop grinding at my brain for something to say, and simply speak my mind.

"Do you miss them? Your family?"

She freezes, and for a moment I expect her to get up and leave. Then she turns to me, cool and dark-eyed.

"Do you?"

"Yes," I say. "Even though they—" My mind flashes with bright fire, and my heart jumps with revolted fear. "Even though they made me leave."

She nods. "Yes," she whispers. "I miss them. I miss all of it."

She takes a deep breath, and her dark eyes close. "I see home all the time, whether I'm awake or asleep. I smell the burning oils; I feel the smooth stone. I see my *parents*..."

She stops, with a shaking breath. I fill the gaping silence. "I understand. My brother—I hear his stories in my head still. I see them in my dreams."

I don't want to tell her about the flames engulfing Hanshen— only the good parts of my dreams, the bittersweet. More than anything, I don't want her to feel alone; my heart rages against her sadness. It wants to embrace her. I can see her glassy eyes, blinking back tears. They're unexpected. I'd never imagined them from her, always a still pool, with only the tiniest ripples.

I must look lost, because she sniffs back any tears she had, and gives me a halfhearted smile. "You haven't been to Cer'ah, have you?"

"Women aren't allowed on boats." I reply instinctively. She bursts out laughing, and it's the most beautiful thing I've ever heard, even dampened by tears.

"Your people are so *strange*." She pulls the pendant of her necklace from her robe, and I recognise it immediately. It's the huge fish scale, glinting bright blue in the moonlight.

"In Cer'ah, no one has heard of the Oakfather." she whispers conspiratorially. "We have dragons."

A jolt of excitement shoots through me. Wonder descends on my imagination like a sudden whirlwind.

"This is a gift from the ruler of our city," she continues, lifting the scale farther into the light. "The dragon Angkasa, the merchant king. It's an heirloom—our family's pride."

I am speechless. *A dragon. A bright city.* Florian told me a little about that, I remember, not long before I left Hanshen—about

necklace from her robe. "You should be proud to take our name, Renate Duskwood."

The pendant is an Oak leaf, carved intricately from wood. Renate accepts the necklace and bows her head to receive it, though there's a little tension in her proffered brow. I see her hand press into her robe, in the space over her heart.

Angkasa's scale lies there.

But I cannot dwell on that. It's my turn.

I stand on the platform, staring out at all of them: Ilse and dark, tall Otto, with their eyes of silent encouragement; Ari and Conrad, filled to the brim with excitement; Leot, smiling, quietly enthusiastic... and Renate, watching. *Always watching.*

The expectation in Engelberta's eyes causes me to shiver from the inside out.

Renate sat. Yes. I'll sit.

I set myself down cross-legged on the platform. It pulls at the muscles in my legs. I never liked sitting like this. I shuffle and shift, trying to find a suitable position.

Engelberta clears her throat.

I tense and then force myself back into a more relaxed posture. With one last glance at the canopy, I squeeze my eyes shut.

I can do this. I'll pretend no one is here.

I think back to the first time the meditation worked. The eagle and its golden eyes—I should remember that. I picture it, down to the smell of the cold twilight and the cadence of the wind. The eagle set itself on my shoulder; it *chose* to be near me.

With the thought of flying, the meditation wavers. The wind sings past like that first day I ran from the beach. I quell it.

Become one with it all. Do that, and unlock something greater.

Engelberta is saying something, but I don't hear it. All there is is twilight and an eagle. All there is is a soft breeze and the wavering silence of the wood.

Time becomes strange.

I am alone, in darkness and in light. Everything has disappeared, and there is only a hollow wind, and me.

But what am I, here? It's not clear. I try to search for the Oakfather, for Rhene, for anyone, but I have no eyes to open.

A voice floats from the back of my mind. *Perhaps you should make some.*

The eagle—golden-eyed, brown-feathered.

Yes. I'll be an eagle.

The moment I make that decision and reach out, I'm thrown back into the world I know.

When I open my eyes, things look different. I am still surrounded, but the people are much taller, and farther away. The lines in their faces are clearer; the quirks in their expressions and the folds of their robes come in multitudes; the bark of the great oak above is made up of so many tiny patterns I can't fathom them. Every leaf lays itself before my gaze; I can even see a bug crawling along a faraway branch.

I want to fly. I don't care about their detailed faces or their cheering; I only want to go up. I must have the sky.

I have wings; I do not need to look. I just need to go up.

Excitement bubbles in my chest as I flap my wings. Somehow it feels as though I've always had them.

I waste no time. I step from the platform.

A winged arrow, I cut a line through the startled crowd and arc immediately back around, sights set on the sunlight bursting through the leaves above. Wind rips past; leaves shiver in my wake.

Then I crash through the canopy and out into the sky, and I soar.

Duskwood rolls out before me in every direction, an ever-growing blanket of green. The greatest thing about it is that it's so far away—I'm embraced by the expanse of the sky. I can finally breathe; the wind is singing in my feathers, and there is no limit to it. There is no salt in the air, and no fear. In absolute exhilaration, I whoop as loud as I can. The breath tears itself out of my joyous beak as a strange squawk—and then I can't stop laughing, which sounds worse. *This must look ridiculous. A laughing, squawking mess of a bird, rolling across the sky.* But it doesn't matter—no one can see me. My weightlessness increases tenfold—right now, this is my sky. I am beautifully, wonderfully alone.

I continue flying, immediately addicted to the wind and wild movement around me. I cannot stop, twisting and shooting around, squawking like a fool all the while.

But soon, amidst my heightening joy, something beneath it is fraying. Worry begins to pool in my chest.

What's happening?

All of a sudden, I can't stop looking back at the forest. My flight path is wobbling slightly; I feel like I'm losing my grip on a rope.

My vision blurs then becomes soft and sharp in quick succession, and I start to get an extremely intrusive feeling that I might have hands, not wings. A snippet of black, like a quick window shutter, flows at soundspeed through my mind, and before I can question anything, I'm falling.

My breathing is heavy. The wind is rushing past but not kindly, not playfully, and my heart won't stop beating; I have hands, and normal-seeing eyes and hair and I'm falling, *I'm falling, I'm—*

I squeeze my eyes shut.

Shapechange back into the eagle. Shapechange back into the eagle.

The canopy is approaching, a terrifying pit of green rising up rapidly to meet me; I brace for the scraping of twigs and the bludgeoning branches, and for the end—I can't possibly survive this, I can't look, *I can't look—*

The pain never comes. Just a thud as I fall into something that is not the ground.

There are arms carrying me. I'm still descending, but slower. I open my eyes and stare up.

It's a... *man?* His eyes are orange, bright against his dark skin. Antlers, like those of the stags from Conrad's sketchbook, protrude from his head, out of auburn hair that rolls down over his shoulders. *And,* I realise, listening to the sweeping wind as we descend, *he has wings.* Gigantic, human-sized wings, bigger than any eagle by many times. They're auburn, like his hair, and ridged with earthy browns.

I want to ask who he is, but the shock of falling paralysed me. My muscles are immovable, and my breath is all gone.

We land beneath the great Oak, to the surprise of all those congregated. He puts me gently down. I stand there, unmoving as a statue. My brain is filled with a strange fuzz.

Renate runs up to me and takes my shoulder. The look on her face forces me to draw back; there's genuine, unconcealed shock.

The others look only at the man with wings.

"Roth!" Engelberta calls, inclining her head. "It's an honour to see you again."

The realisation hits me like a sharp gust of wind.

This is Roth Duskwood: the founder of this place.

I didn't know if I'd ever meet him; in Conrad's stories he sounded like an adventurer, searching for something great in faraway lands. But there he stands, stranger than I could ever imagine. His face is neither young nor old; even without the antlers and wings, I've never seen anyone like him. Renate stares alongside me.

Roth soon turns from his conversation with Engelberta and looks to us, his orange eyes alight with a strangely distant sympathy. Engelberta clears her throat, and proffers another beaded necklace.

"The one you saved is called Kestra. Kestra Duskwood."

That name sounds strange next to mine. It's like Engelberta's talking about someone different—someone important; someone impressive. Nonetheless, the pride in her bright green eyes still makes my heart glow.

I don't have time to dwell on any ponderous thoughts of inadequacy, anyway. I'm caught in Roth's intimidating shadow, and the hawkishness of his watching eyes.

"Thank you," I blurt out, bowing to him in the customary way.

"There is no need," he rumbles, inclining his head in return. His voice is smooth and deep, like earth and water mixing.

Then, simply, he turns back to his conversation, and we are all left to disperse.

That night, there is feasting in honour of Roth's return—

Otto creates the best meal I've ever had, and we celebrate as though the night will never end.

Strangely, Roth does not join us. Neither does Engelberta. Nevertheless, amongst the revelry, it feels like we're not really missing them.

Someone—Folkera, I think, one of the older druids, with long golden hair—is playing a wooden flute. Conrad can't stop chattering about the events of the morning. Ari and Leot are getting their first taste of the delicious honey mead that another of the older druids produced—Matthias, who already appears very drunk, with great crumbs of half-eaten food stuck haphazardly in his beard—and Ilse is looking on like a harried mother, despite being equal to her friends in age. The scene makes me chuckle into my own cup of mead, and even earns a twitch of amusement from Renate's mouth.

She is quiet, as usual. As we laugh and talk as freely as we ever have, though, I see a smile come into her face more and more.

When the celebrations begin to wind down, she looks at me. I feel the trail of her eyes on my skin, flickering in their intensity. When no one is close enough hear, she speaks.

"To the glade?" she whispers.

In that moment, I'd like nothing more.

12

WE ARE STUMBLING SHADOWS, moving as quietly as we can through the wood. Tonight, the moon is cloaked—and so Duskwood is shrouded in darkness. Echoes of revelling druids float from behind us.

The glade. It shouldn't be that far away. But it's so dark. I can't...

Despite my tiredness, an idea occurs to me like a bright spark. I sit down with a rustle in the undergrowth, and I hear the swishing of Renate's robes as she turns back to me. I can imagine the look on her face exactly— familiar, veiled confusion.

"What are you doing?" she hisses, and then there's a little worry in the tone of her voice. "Are you alright?"

"Just wait," I reply.

There's less going on now, so it's much easier to reach the right space, tucked away in my mind. I hear the forest; I see the eagle. That was *me*. I was something else, but still myself. I can be that again, easily. Those eyes—*my* eyes, but different—could see through this darkness easily.

It's surprising how fast I transform. Time seems to slow, but I control it. One moment, I'm at peace, completely alone in the sweeping blankness of my mind, and then I have wings, and the forest is lighter than before. I can see Renate next to me, in the process of reaching out to check where I am.

I caw as quietly as I can and flap up into the low tree branches. The night shadows are no longer a burden.

I know the way.

I hop from branch to branch, leading her by the rustling of the leaves and an occasional, tentative caw. Even in the dark of Duskwood's night, it seems as though we make it in no time.

I watch from above as she stumbles into the grassy sea of the glade. She laughs, the tone full and genuine. My heart stops; it's all I can hear. Whenever she laughs, I feel like I do when I fly—caught in the dance of singing, wonderful wind.

"You did it, Kestra." she calls up to me. "You can come down now."

She's squinting, not quite seeing in the darkness. I'm still catching myself, struggling not to fall off of the branch I'm perched on.

"Alright," she says. "Thank you. Will you come down now?"

She thinks I'm being stubborn. It's so funny I have to stifle the squawking that passes for a laugh in this form.

I barrel down into the grass and let the soft impact jolt me back into myself. When I look up, I can see the faint shape of her hand reaching out from the shadows. I try to grab it, but miss the first time, swinging wide with splayed fingers.

"Sorry," I say, "Can't see a thing now."

"That eagle can, though."

"Would you rather—?"

"No, you idiot. I want someone who can talk. It's just a matter of light."

The stupidest idea I've ever had pops into my head.

After I think about it for a moment, though, perhaps it's less stupid than I thought. Though I can barely see her, Renate is there, strong and enigmatic and terrifying, but *trustworthy*.

I can trust her—why?

I don't know at all. I'm only sure she's different from everyone I've ever met. That's enough.

"I can make light." I say simply.

She takes a breath, and the air between us feels thick.

"Go on, then," she says. I can hear the goading smirk in her voice, but it's safe, somehow.

We sit down together. My bones are trembling at their core. There's no backing down now. I hold my hand out—though neither of us can see—and I wait for my anger, the kindling and the spark. I can't find it. I'm here with Renate, and my chest is light. Instead of rage, there's a swelling, blooming sensation inside me.

So that's what I focus on.

The fire comes quickly, with a satisfying burst of triumph. It's followed by instinctual fear, in the excruciating wait for Renate's response.

"Interesting," she remarks. She pats me on the shoulder and loops her arm behind my neck as she gazes, face flickering in the soft light. "Well done."

My finger glows stronger with a bright flame. There is silence.

She knows this is sinful and wrong, and yet she stares like it's beautiful. On the other hand, all I can see is her.

I made the flame without anger. *What does that mean?* Perhaps it was just in the triumph of the day—a simple fluke. It felt right, though—making it from triumph. From whatever I'm feeling on this day, with Renate.

I remain silent, pondering for a while. Renate does too, staring deep into the flame. I'm scared that she'll suddenly realise this is all wrong—that I'm a destroyer, committing a sin against the Oakfather's way—but my heart knows better. She's different from Otto and Conrad, in a good way. Her mind is freer, detached from the confines of this sanctuary. The peace of the church is wonderful, but it seems that someone like me cannot be entirely peaceful, with this evil flame inside me. Renate sees that and doesn't seem to care.

"Thank you," I say out of nowhere, after we've been sitting in my flame's meagre light for a while.

"What for?" she replies.

"For seeing this flaw, and... being kind about it."

The shame is coming back, but I force myself not to look away. Her face is mostly blank, though there's a furrow of confusion in her brow.

"It's not a flaw. You can make light. You're like the sun."

An all encompassing ache assaults my heart. It's terrible and wonderful. I have no words.

"It's like the way water comes to me," she continues. "From what Conrad said, all of this seems like any other set of skills — you're naturally better at some than others."

I nod slowly. It makes sense. It does.

Something in the back of my mind doesn't want it to be.

A night breeze sweeps through the glade, ruffling my strange candle and our hair. Mine sweeps over her, long and wild as ever, but she doesn't flinch away.

Nevertheless, there's an emptiness in our space; I can feel it coming out of her. Her words are still ringing. They're turning over and over in her head.

She sighs. "I suppose it's strange that I was immediately so attuned to the thing that killed everyone I love."

A pang hits me, and the flame flickers. But I make it brighter and brighter, until I'm holding it in my hand; it's a small fire, now.

I remember how she looked, almost dead. Then blank, at the news of their deaths.

"But *you* didn't kill them," I whisper. "And," I pause. It's like something's stuck fast in my throat. "The way you move the water. Sometimes I think it's the most wonderful thing I've ever seen."

She's silent. My heart is beating faster than a hummingbird's wings. I think I hear her sniff back tears.

"Well," she says, and there's a tremor in her voice. "What I'm seeing right now, dancing in your hand—what's that, if not beautiful?"

She gestures to the fire. It's comfortable, not too hot against my palm—like a mug of something warm, comforting and safe in its heat. We huddle closer. My heart won't stop, beating and beating and beating. She tentatively pulls her arm around me, and my face becomes as warm as my palm. I can feel her breath against my cheek, and her soft hair on my neck as she leans against it...

There's a loud rustle behind us, deafening in the silence. My heart jolts up with my body. I turn around, stupidly brandishing my flaming hand and see the face of Conrad staring back at me, eyes wide.

I snuff the flame immediately, balling my hand into a tight fist.

"I'm sorry," I whisper frantically, "I can explain."

I feel Renate's presence behind me. *She agrees with me. She'll help. I just have to explain to Conrad, I just have to make him understand—*

"I..." Conrad croaks. He sounds shaken. "You know what Engelberta said—you knew, right? You must've known..."

I can't see him properly, but his breaths are erratic. He's panicking, and I want to help, I do, *but how do I...*

"Repent," he says desperately, like he's parroting something important he learned. He's suddenly pulling himself together, but he still seems childlike in his nervousness. Despite my fear, I feel for him. "Repent. Please, just... Let's forget about this. I don't want you to be—" He stops abruptly and gulps. Then he whispers:

"It was an accident, right?"

I nod hurriedly, then realise he can't see. "Yes."

My throat is dry. I'd never considered properly what Engelberta would do to someone like me—I just knew she could never know.

I don't want to destroy. Maybe if I just talked to her—

I stop myself. I remember the punishment for people who were different in Hanshen. I remember the cold grime of the Hold and the taste of bitter salt on the freezing air. This place is peaceful and warm and kind, but there's an undercurrent of something else.

Those who destroy must be destroyed, Engelberta said.

104

I was trying not to think about it, but I know what that means. I've known this whole time.

I will not be destroyed, so I pull Conrad into a hug and profess that I am sorry. Not for what I did, though something in my mind still echoes that sentiment—*destroyer, destroyer*—but for putting him in this position. For upsetting him.

"It's alright," I say. "It was a stupid mistake. I'll never do it again."

He leans into me, so short in comparison to my height, and tightens the hug, like he's a sailor clinging to the wreckage of his ship. My heart is cracking, frozen with fear then hit hard with the fact that Conrad is just a child, like us. Engelberta raised him to feel this way.

We return to the sanctuary in silence, but Conrad seems to have calmed, despite his shakiness. He explained that he saw us leave, and got lonely when Otto started a different conversation with Folkera and Matthias. He just wondered where we were going, that was all.

The whole way back, Renate's fingers keep brushing mine. Just before we reach the lights of the church, our fingers are entwined. Then she pulls away, and I see the ghost of a comforting smile brush her face in the half-light.

As we enter the light, and her silhouette moves in front of me, I steady myself.

Things will be alright. With Renate here, things will be alright.

13

WE CONTINUE AS NORMAL. The seasons change again, from Spring to Summer to Autumn. Duskwood is wreathed in reds and browns; in the harsh morning sunlight it burns with orange and yellow. *Like fire.*

About a month after Conrad discovered my fire, Renate convinced me to start training with her, secretly. She's shrewd about it—the way she sees it, it's better if Engelberta and the older druids don't know exactly what we're capable of, in case we both have to run at short notice.

Her control of water is more incredible than I ever could have imagined. She's even been playing around with changing the temperature. Sometimes, with enough focus, she can make her jewels of water into shards of ice, straight from the air.

Whenever we go to the glade to practise or have some quiet, we make doubly sure Conrad doesn't see us. I feel a biting pain in my heart whenever we go—I don't want to see him upset, and I fear death, or exile, or whatever Engelberta might have in store for me if she found out. And yet I can't get rid of the flame inside me, despite the threat. The sessions are guilty occasions, but they're also the most exciting part of the day, or week, or month, depending on when we can get away. It's great to have Renate there for many reasons, but also in case of a loss of control on my part; she's always ready to pluck water from the air and solve the problem of any burning trees. I never seem to lose control the way I did before, though—as soon as I make a flame bigger than the one on that night we were found out, I remember the house. I still see my family's terror in my mind.

I miss them. I can barely picture their faces now, just their eyes, reflecting bright fire. Florian's stories haven't left me, but they've been dulled by time. Their forms are grey and ghostlike now—except for one. The bright cities he spoke about have become Renate's, vivid as ever in my dreams.

Dreams. Hanshen still burns in those.

I often wonder, after a session of maintaining a strong, safe flame, whether this thing could be used for good. It makes warmth, after all. And light.

Renate told me about special mountains called volcanoes— her family visited one together in Cer'ah. Volcanoes have liquid fire at their cores, so fire might be part of the Oakfather's natural world, just like the other elements.

Nevertheless, outside the glade I must let the thoughts rest, and focus on the things I can do without fear.

Otto continues to teach me about the peace I need to find when shapechanging and speaking to nature. Animals are becoming easier to understand, though the chickens milling around the sanctuary remain as simple as ever.

Animals are like us, Otto says, with minds built from the same mould. Plants, however, and trees—those are difficult to understand. I have to become completely quiet inside, and even then, when I catch a snatching of something, it's more like a feeling or a vague idea. Otto sees their messages in images, like vivid dreams flashing across his mind.

I will learn in time, he says. With enough practice, I will learn.

To my daily relief, Engelberta has been absent more often than not. I tentatively ask Conrad about it. He tells me that her illness is worsening.

"The smoke of her childhood doesn't ever seem to leave her," he says. "You can hear it in her coughing."

He doesn't look at me, instead fixing his eyes on the ground. I offer him a hug all the same. He accepts, wordlessly.

"She's finding healing in the wood," he mumbles into my chest. "She'll be alright. I know she will."

With Engelberta absent and Roth long gone—he only stayed for a day, then disappeared like smoke—the sanctuary feels thin.

Perhaps this is my time to understand. For so many months, I've felt like a shadow, stumbling around in a forest of ignorance. I remember walking into the church for the first time and wondering what was on the upper floors of the tower. Now I know that it's where Engelberta resides. *But if she's not here, perhaps...*

. . .

In the folds of late afternoon, when everyone is out and the space is clear around the church, I enter.

The rooms above are simpler than I expected. There's a hammock—Engelberta's, I assume—and plain furniture. In one room I find a desk, with papers strewn on it. In another there seems to be storage—great wooden chests line the walls. Thankfully, none of them have locks. One of them is marked with a particularly pretty engraving of an oak leaf.

I can't resist.

Inside are books, covers written in a similar script to Conrad's sketchbook notes. In fact, when I open one of them, it looks much the same. Drawings of different lands and animals and things I can't even begin to guess at fill the pages.

Certain sketches catch my eye. There's one of a leaf, and next to it a tree, with a scale that seems to suggest it's almost a hundred times larger than a normal tree. 'World Tree', a note reads beside it. I don't know what to make of that, so I examine the other drawing. It's an oak leaf, carefully conveyed—I could trace each vein and imperfection for hours. It's as though the leaf is really there, broad yet oddly delicate.

I flip through the book some more and catch an image that seems familiar. A beast, with layers upon layers of scales and great horns. Ridges run along its back, from its majestic head to the tip of its tail, and it has wings, big enough to cloak its entire body.

Renate tried to draw a picture of Angkasa in the dirt, once. It wasn't great, but it had the same sort of silhouette. At the bottom of the page, artfully scrawled, is the word 'Dragon'. The drawing is so detailed that I can't help but believe I'm seeing a true representation. *Yes. This is what they look like, then.*

On the opposite page lies something curious. My love of the form of the eagle sparks when I see it: *a bird of some kind, but...*

Its wings are ablaze.

No. That can't be right.

'Phoenix', it reads. I've never heard of it, though even uncoloured its eyes seem to be alight, roaring with fire. I study its form, unable to take my eyes off it. Every curve of every feather; the hook of its beak; the patterns the flames make on its wings—all of it burns, searing itself into my memory.

Shaking myself out of whatever curious trance I got myself into, I search the books and box for any indication of who they belong to—*they can't be Engelberta's, can they?* That flaming bird wasn't something she'd ever want to study.

After a few minutes of further scouring, I notice an additional engraving on the box, in the bottom left corner. 'Roth Duskwood' it reads. The elusive Roth, with his wings and antlers and deep orange eyes.

Are these records of his journeys?

I pack everything away and attempt to arrange things exactly as they were. I avoided the desk in the other room before, certain it was Engelberta's—but I can't any more. I'm missing something— I need to understand why she feels this way about people like me. If I can finally understand, this snooping could be the most important thing I've ever done.

The papers strewn about the desk seem uninteresting, though a map of Duskwood and its surroundings does catch my eye. I've never really studied a map properly before—back in Hanshen, they were tools of the fishermen only, so even a glimpse by anyone else was frowned upon.

Hanshen is on this map, a tiny northern dot at the tip of the land. Duskwood is vast, sprawling across the entire mass of land above the Spires. A little ways beneath that mountain range, I see Brennof, which lies tucked into a rough curve of the land, beneath the rocky islands that scatter from the Spires in a line between the Rhenesee and the Hallesee. The journeys Florian made, though few, look dangerous from this perspective. I can imagine one jagged rock tearing through our wooden boats and spelling the end for them all.

There are drawers in the desk, which I can't help but slide open. In one, I find a thick book. I open it and begin flicking through. Writing, more writing—it seems like it's some kind of journal. Perfect—something in here has to be important; *there has to be something here, something to explain—*

Something catches my eye. 'Settlement reclaimed'.

The entry is dated well over a decade ago. Beside it, there's a sketch of the map, with a cross drawn on a place north of the sanctuary. If I had to guess, my path should have crossed it on my way in, but the only people I've seen have been here.

I don't think there are any other places like the church—they haven't been mentioned, at least. Noting my curiosity for later, I read on, hungry for information.

'17 casualties. 2 viable recruits. Trade was made with a surviving resident on condition of exile: young child acquired— male, brown hair, hazel eyes, freckled, rather small...'

I don't know why, but I suddenly feel sick. Confusion is spiralling through my mind - *casualties? Recruits?* I don't know what those mean specifically, but I'm sure of one thing: the child being described is Conrad. It has to be. *The ages line up, and the appearance, down to the last detail...*

'On condition of exile', someone gave him up. *Conrad's*

mother? What was the danger, and why was a child the price? It doesn't make sense. *Why a child?* The sickness inside me begins to rise, developing into a creeping feeling that I can't ignore.

And then it begins to occur to me. *Who didn't come here as a child?* I don't think of myself as one now, but it's been two years. When I came here, I was a child. It was the same with Renate, Ari, Leot, Ilse, Otto, and, apparently, Conrad.

A 'viable recruit'. I ponder the phrase. *Is that what children are? If so, then casualties are adults.*

But who creates the casualties?

I take a breath. Deep down, I know.

Engelberta, at the very least. Maybe some of the older members. *Matthias. Folkera. Otto?*

I hope it's not true; I hope with all my heart. But here, on paper, it seems that to 'reclaim' a settlement is to wipe it out.

I sit there, languishing in a sickening silence. Engelberta's mind has only become more of an enigma. *Fire is not allowed because it destroys, and yet the 'reclamation' of Duskwood settlements is justified?*

I don't know what to think—I must be missing something. I just want it all to be untrue, somehow. I decide not to read on, for fear of having even more questions. I put everything back into its rightful place, and with a final glance to the desk, I tear myself away and sneak out of the church.

But I can't forget it. Even as I walk out into the evening glow of the sanctuary, my mind is like a hive of bees, buzzing with unwanted thoughts. My shoulders feel as though something heavy has been placed on them, and can never be taken off.

I have to think about this, yes. But when I next see Engelberta, how can I ever be silent? I have to ask questions—in such a way that she won't suspect what I did, or what I am.

It feels like an impossible task.

Days pass. Autumn finishes blooming and dies like fire. With Engelberta gone and Conrad's mind focused fully on her illness, Renate and I spend more time in the glade. Renate's precision—with every element, not just water—is becoming astounding. She can harness vast amounts of wind and knock me off my feet with a sly chuckle, and right after can separate a ball of water into thousands of little jewels without batting an eye.

My flames are coming easier and easier. Whenever I'm with Renate, there's this strange undercurrent of joy within me, like fuel for my fire. Instead of feeling drained by overusing my power, I find myself energised. I don't seem to need anger—I can produce more controllable flame by utilising something else. It helps me to keep thoughts of Engelberta's journals out of my mind; instead, I revel in fire, imagining myself as that bright flaming bird from Roth's sketchbooks.

At Renate's request, I explain to her how the process of creating flame has changed. Ever curious, she tries to replicate it.

I watch her struggle—it's strange, she never really seems to struggle as much as me with anything, but here, it's like she's fighting an impossible battle. After almost a day of attempting to muster any kind of flame, she manages it—the tiniest candle-flame, flickering from her index finger. As soon as it appears, she winces.

"...hurts," she hisses.

The flame soon goes out. Her dark hair has been ruffled by the day's strong winds, and her skin is moist with sweat.

"Well," she says, with an exasperated sigh. "At least it might be useful as a children's magic trick when I go home."

A pang strikes my chest. *Right, she's going home. That's partly why we're doing this.*

I keep trying to forget. Sometimes I fear waking up and finding her gone. It's irrational, I know. She'd tell me. I know she would.

So I calm myself and offer her my hand. We return to the sanctuary again, bathed in twilight.

14

Engelberta hasn't returned for days. Conrad looks like he's fraying at the edges, and I can't wait much longer. My questions are busting out of me.

No one I ask seems to know where exactly she is—not even the older druids.

When I approach Otto, he doesn't seem surprised at my request.

"With your permission, can I go and search for Engelberta?"

Otto frowns. "I have a feeling you'll do it even if I don't give my permission." he says, side-eyeing me suspiciously.

His sternness is broken by signs of worry, scattered haphazardly in his face. Worry for me? For Engelberta? I don't know. After what I discovered, I can't be sure what anyone here truly thinks any more.

After a moment, he nods. "Alright. It's about time we started looking, if I'm honest." Another pause. "Just... Take the others, won't you? And stay airborne where you can—the bears don't much like it when we don't keep to our territory."

I nod.

As soon as I propose the plan, Conrad is ready to go immediately. Renate takes one look at me and nods slowly, tentative.

She's calculating. Always calculating.

"Where first?" she soon asks.

"I have a few ideas," Conrad blurts out. He begins listing places Engelberta took him as a child, and pilgrimage spots she had spoken of—safe hollows of Duskwood where druids can avoid disturbing the angrier denizens of the Oakfather's wood.

I find that timeless, quiet place in my mind and become an eagle before I know it. Conrad swiftly transforms as well, into one with tawny feathers similar to mine. The form of Renate's is unexpected; it has the right shape, but it's like she's painted it, deciding exactly what colour everything should be, with no care for the hues of the animals in Duskwood. Her feathers are sleek and dark, and they have a faint blue shimmer to them. Her eyes, which I expected to be dark, are pale, bright as a river in Winter.

I never realised we didn't have to copy animals exactly when shapechanging—I make a mental note to try it later.

And so we set off, shooting through the canopy like arrows and breaking into the cool blue of the early Winter sky. The trees are mostly bare below us, but the wind still sings past in its beautiful, familiar way; the sky is welcoming me back—*this time, I won't fall from it. I won't let myself.*

As we fly, it becomes apparent that Conrad is a good leader, considering we can't speak whilst shapechanged. His wing movements are minute but pointed—he leads us in due course to each place that he listed before we set off. Each time we approach one, we glide lower and lower, slowing slightly as we break through the canopy—though still remaining securely above ground with the immense height of Duskwood's trees.

Three pairs of eagle eyes, yet no Engelberta. As the sun begins to climb to its apex, we're getting tired. Each time we are greeted by an empty place, this strange burden grows heavier on my shoulders, and the questioning fire grows fiercer in my heart. *We have to find her. I need answers.*

We're approaching a section of the wood that seems quite far north. I can tell in the others' dogged wing beats that they're exhausted, too. We're all coming to terms with returning empty handed.

We break the canopy for what feels like the thousandth time. Initially, there's nothing. The same naked trees, made dull by Winter, whooshing past in their masses, until...

There she is. A beacon of tranquil green in the distance, framed against the sundrenched bones of some long-ruined settlement.

She's there. She's really there. Conrad speeds up towards her, and she turns immediately at the sound. In the flurry of the moment, my determined fire sickens; even with Renate close by me I suddenly don't know what to ask. As an eagle, I cannot talk, but if I could there would be nothing falling from my lips.

Conrad shapechanges rapidly and embraces Engelberta.

It elicits a coughing fit worse than I've ever heard from her.

Duskwood's healing couldn't do much for her, after all.

A stream of questions and trembling, happy babbling is coming from Conrad's mouth. I'd feel joy at seeing their reunion, but considering what I've learnt over the past few days, I don't know what to feel.

Renate and I walk up slowly. Engelberta is nodding at Conrad, but only giving him short answers, it seems. She returns his hug with a faltering smile, then looks away towards the village carcass that engulfs the forest ahead.

In this moment, I can't see her face. *What is her expression? Is she mournful? Does she revel in the memory of destruction?*

She is the reason for this gigantic skeleton. Her and... *others.* I don't want to imagine Otto doing anything like this. Leaving casualties. Acquiring recruits. He is a little younger than Matthias and Folkera, so maybe he hasn't taken part in this. *I hope he hasn't.*

Engelberta looks back at Conrad once more. The set of her face is complicated. There's a coolness, and a warmth. There's the absentminded stare of memory.

With a deep sickness in my heart, I admit it to myself. *It's all true.* This place—it's the one that I crossed once before, on my terrified way from Hanshen. I had imagined warm food cooking, smoke coming out of one of the ruined chimneys. People working —perhaps even a small child, taking his first steps. I can't help but glance at Conrad. Then I shake it from my mind. When Conrad was taken, he probably couldn't even walk yet.

Something's still bothering me. If all the other adults were killed, why not Conrad's mother? Why not just take him instead of making a deal? That's another question I have to get answered somehow.

When we arrive from our distant approach, Engelberta fixes us with a stare. I no longer know what to say. Only sickness and hopeless confusion rule me now.

"Good. You two are here as well."

I have to say something. Anything at all, I—

"What happened here?" Renate asks, staring round at the

skeletal village remains. Relief floods through my bones. *I'm not alone.*

Engelberta is silent. Her face darkens, and the moment seems to stretch on forever.

"Many years ago, the Oakfather's hand came down in retribution. It was to cleanse Duskwood, once and for all." she begins.

As she pauses to take a breath, a hacking cough rips through her. It lasts too long. Frozen panic shifts in the air; none of us know what to do. Everything is hushed. The wind whistles emptily through the trees.

Then she recovers, and rights herself.

"Druids are guardians. Of Duskwood especially, but also the rest of the natural world. Our burden is great. To protect this place and ensure the world will live on, sacrifices must be made."

Renate is silent. Not in her usual, calculating way—I can see it in her face. She is stunned.

"You mean—"

"Renate." Engelberta snaps. "I have seen what happens when men who do not respect the land we walk on have their way. They don't stop. They *never* stop. Not until the skies are black with smoke, and their fires burn eternally, crushing those that stoke them—"

"But to kill people—" Renate begins.

"The end the Oakfather grants is merciful—" Engelberta breaks down into a coughing fit again. Conrad, as though not hearing any of her words, steadies her, patting her on the back. She gestures to herself, and speaks hoarsely:

"This is the other death. The one that many will face, and have faced." She pauses, sucking in a breath. "The choking hand of smoke will strangle us all, quickly or slowly, if we don't work to make the world a better place."

"There has to be some other way," Renate interjects. "You could teach people about these problems instead, they'd all want to fix them—"

Engelberta fixes her with an exhausted gaze.

"I'm disappointed, Renate. You should understand by now." she reprimands. "It would not be done if it did not have to be. Children are still able to learn—and you have been taught the right way. For those who are grown and already bent into unchanging shape, there is no hope. Death is a mercy."

Renate does not reply.

My mind is running faster than a rushing river. *So, the 'viable recruits' in her journal* were *children.* That truth rings out loud and clear in my head. Adults are too far gone, she said. Otto's father, then, who starved to death in the woods and was 'found' by Engelberta... *No. I won't think about it. I can't bear it.* That adults can't learn—it can't be true. *When I'm older, I'll still be able to learn new things, I'm sure of it. I'll still be able to change.*

Then my mother's face flashes unwanted through my head.

She cared more about Rhene than me. The execution of her daughter didn't provoke anything to change in her. Not one tiny thing. But there is only one of her. Not everyone is the way she is. *Engelberta can't be right. She can't be.*

She's begun coughing again, steadied by Conrad. He doesn't seem fazed by any of this. When she spoke, he simply nodded along, as though it all made sense.

"Never mind this," Engelberta says. "You will all understand as you grow. Perhaps one day, you will see what I've seen. But for now we must focus on the Oakfather, and Duskwood."

An air of foreboding surrounds her words. My blood is running hot into my face and rushing painfully through my head. *This is wrong, all of this. It has to be.*

"In my recent journey, I have seen terrible things." Engelberta declares. "The northern village—the last of its kind—has begun defacing Duskwood."

My stomach drops. *Hanshen. I never imagined they would... What about the Path?* A terrible, ugly mixture of emotion is rising within me: anger, hatred, sorrow, all tugging me in their separate directions.

Hanshen burns; I see it again before me.

"Old, sacred trees are being felled fast. Too fast. With some of the timber, they're not even building. The plumes of smoke from their bonfires rise higher by the day as they burn away space for their fields. Something must be done."

She turns away from us, lost in the skeleton before her.

"For the Oakfather's life to flourish, the remainder of this land must be cleansed."

Words do not rise in my throat—only sickness.

Renate finds me after we return, curled into my hammock. My mind is buzzing. I couldn't confront Engelberta; I don't even know how I feel about ending the people that tried to end me. *The destruction of Hanshen? It's what I've been seeing—but is it what I fear or what I want?*

She taps me on the shoulder and I look up into her dark eyes. I take a breath, ready to reluctantly try to explain how I feel.

She knows what's in my heart already.

"We'll run away." she says. I do not respond. At her careful glances, I can imagine the pitiful, dull hopelessness in my face.

She sits down next to me, and we sway limply in the hammock.

"I won't be part of it." she continues. "And, come on. You know I was never going to stay here. Were you?"

That familiar pang at the thought of her leaving hits me. I don't know. It was nice to have a home, even if I was still afraid. *But if Renate and I left together...*

"We could fly South, in the night." she whispers, eyes wide. "All day, until we can see the Spires, rising up out of the earth against the dawn. Then we'll fly over them, too, and make it to Brennof, or wherever the closest port is. Then..."

She falters, and I recognise the terrifying crash of the sea in her frozen gaze.

So I pick her imaginary journey up, and clutch her hand.

"Then we'll go together across the Hallesee. Water can't kill the person you've become. You're too powerful. Nothing will stand in your way."

She squeezes my hand back and nods, with a quiet breath.

"And we'll be safe," she whispers, "because we'll be together."

15

The days of Winter creep by like slow-crawling ants.

Renate and I have started filling the old woven pack I brought with me when I arrived here. Even now, the musty, faded smell reminds me of Florian, and of home. I don't know why I still think of Hanshen as my home, even as its burning rooftops rage within my mind.

Everything we need will be in the pack.

Enough food. Not dried, like the stash I had in my first journey through Duskwood, but as long-lasting as possible. After that runs out, we'll have to hunt. It shouldn't be trouble with our shapechanging abilities, but I'm not taking anything for granted. Though it was almost a year ago now, my fall from the sky is fresh in my memory.

There are fresh sets of clothes, including our old ones, which will appear more normal when we enter civilisation, Renate says. The greens and browns of our robes are normal enough, but to be dressed exactly the same as each other would seem strange. I just nod along. I've never been to a big city, but she's from one—if there's one thing I'm sure of, it's her understanding of it all.

She thinks of everything. The more we plan, the more it is evident that she's been thinking about this from the day she first got here.

And yet I can't stop feeling like an ocean, jostled and spitting at the slightest upset. There is a buzz in the sanctuary—it seems most have heard what we must do.

The majority of them have probably 'cleansed' before. It makes me feel sick; day in, day out, my insides won't stop trembling.

Horribly, Otto is as serene as ever. I remember his words.

Sometimes, people must die for the wood to live.

I don't speak to him, and don't eat as much of his food. Although it smells wonderful, as always, it turns sour in my mouth. I can tell he's worried about me, but I *won't* speak to him. If he can do this without question, he's beyond saving.

Mercifully, it seems we're not alone in our questions. Ari also has a noticeable anxiety about them. Renate and I see them huddled with Leot, away from the older druids. They both whisper in low voices; a barely perceptible tide of nervousness fluctuates around them. *They're talking it out—trying to understand, the way we tried to. They must be.*

Ilse, on the other hand, seems to already have come to the same conclusion as us—that this can't be right at all. Every time the other two are chattering nervously, she always seems to be looking on sadly into nothing. Whenever I speak to her, the melancholy undertone of her words always seems to be asking why this has to be done. It's permeating her very being.

Engelberta has been watching all of us younger druids,

hawklike. To pacify her, Renate has pretended to come around to the idea of attacking Hanshen—I keep going to the word Engelberta uses, cleansing, but an attack is what it really is. *A massacre, probably.* They'll stand no chance; we control the very elements of the world they inhabit.

My family are ghosts that haunt my dreams more and more—I toss and turn every night in troubled sleep. I've almost always fallen from my hammock by morning.

Our escape looms ahead of us. We practise with our favoured elements.

Our control of the wind was beautiful and freeing, but now I see how it could break bones. People are fragile; they fall easily. They can be thrown.

Renate's water was wonderful to behold, but as I watch her move, I can see how she could suffocate someone without a second thought. Her ocean is not only deadly, but moveable. *If she really wanted it, people could drown.*

And Conrad's earth. It's a good representation of him, steadfast and loyal. But I don't have to imagine what harm his power could wreak; I can already see it. He makes walls of hard earth rise up from nothing. He shakes the ground with a single touch. He terrifies me; it's as though a giant has awoken deep beneath the earth every time he moves.

I remember him the way he was, kind and warm—my first friend in this place. He saved my life without my asking.

Engelberta probably told him to.

No. I know deep down that he would've saved me whether she mentioned it or not. He's *kind.* I can't imagine him doing what he's preparing to do.

Yet there's a fire in his eyes when Engelberta speaks. It's as though he's gone and nothing but her anger remains.

I stand in the cold training grove at the end of practice. Traces of snow and frost coat the world; everything is ice.

I have to tell Conrad the truth about what happened to him. Even if, ultimately, I'm running from Engelberta, I have to speak to him.

"What's wrong?" he asks. It hurts to look at him without telling him the truth.

"I learnt something," I begin, "about Engelberta."

A coolness seeps into him, but he's not all gone.

I have to tell him. It's for his own good.

"You see what we're preparing to do now?"

He nods. I take a breath.

"She's done this before. You know that?"

He nods again. I wince, and try to introduce the idea as gently as I can.

"What are the orders of the attack?"

"Cleanse the village and let its inhabitants be sacrificed for the good of Duskwood. Spare the children, for they can learn to be like us—"

"That's right. Spare the children, recruit them. Teach them the ways."

I don't want to tell him outright, but he's still blank, even as I lay it out. My heart clings to itself, folding inwards. *I have to be direct.*

"Where do you think you came from, Conrad?"

He doesn't respond. I pause again, and breathe. Just breathe. *It's now or never.*

"She took you," I say, "From your mother. It was a deal; if she could have you, she'd let your mother live, as long as she left Duskwood—"

"Don't lie." Conrad says. His voice wobbles a little. "She cared for me when no one else would—"

My palms are warm; a red desperation is beginning to consume me.

"But your mother would have, if you hadn't been taken—"

"No! It's not true! How would *you* know, anyway? You're just angry your home has to be cleansed. You—"

He cuts himself off, looking as though I've just stabbed him in the back. His breaths are rapid and heavy.

I feel the desperation too; I'm losing someone I never truly had to begin with. He takes a deep, angry breath, ready to shoot me down again. A spark goes off within me before he can speak, bright and distraught.

"It's all true!" I yell, knowing nothing else to do. "You just don't want to believe it!"

Fire. It erupts from my hand. I didn't mean to do it, but there it is. I am caught in that moment, suddenly bereft of all anger. There is only slowed time, and cold shock, in my heart and in Conrad's face.

He's right. I *am* angry.

I don't want to destroy Hanshen, and he has to know the truth. He *can't* stay by Engelberta's side knowing what she's done. Surely, he can't—

But he turns and storms away.

127

I quickly snuff out my hand, heart racing like a drum. Eyes narrowed, I search for any prying silhouettes around me.

There is nothing but the wind, singing emptily through the grove. I am alone.

They embark tomorrow.

Renate and I will also be leaving, though we'll be earlier and quieter, heading in the opposite direction entirely.

Evening is beginning to fall. Exhausted from frayed nerves and anticipation and mandatory training in the cold, Renate and I lie in one hammock, intertwined like flowering vines.

We could fall asleep like this, now, and wake before dawn. We could leave in the darkness, hand in hand. We could forget all of this, and be only with each other.

Ever since I could run from things, I have. It's the freest feeling in the world, to leave your shackles behind. But a darkness lies in the pit of my chest, and I know it won't go away.

Not unless I confront Engelberta.

I turn my face to Renate's and feel her soft sleeping breath against my skin.

I don't wake her, sliding from the hammock like a shadow. With one last look, I tear my eyes from the room.

The walk to the church feels slower than it's ever been. The sanctuary feels empty; everyone's inside, out of the harshness of Winter. The leaves have long fallen from the sky, leaving a cracked grey mirror above me. Clouds and frost twist in tandem with black branches. Every tree is a corpse, hung with ice. The cold fights to permeate my bones as the last glimmering rays of white sun dip out of vision.

Ari and Leot stand before the great Oak. Usually, they would be chatting nervously, but now there's a heavy silence in the air as they stand motionless in the harsh cold. As my boots crunch up the path, Leot turns, eyes as blue and frozen as the icicles that hang above us.

We do not exchange words. I just stand with them awhile, looking up alongside them, trying to see what their sad eyes see.

This is probably goodbye, though they don't know that yet.

In a mirror of the time Ari supported me, I pat both of them on the shoulder and leave, continuing my journey to the church.

The trudging of my boots in the snow is a constant rhythm. I lean into it, letting it ground me. *I have to do this.*

The church looms, tall and dark before me. I enter, and my footsteps are loud, echoing in a hollow, barren silence. I make my way up the steps and the creaking of the wooden stairs makes me wince. I push through it. *I will do this.*

As I approach the level of Engelberta's room, I hear talking. My footsteps slow to a stop, and I crouch in the stairwell, straining my ears.

One of the voices is Conrad's:

"I'm sorry I didn't tell you sooner—" he stutters, "I was scared, just scared—"

"It's alright, child." Engelberta responds. Though her voice is hoarse, her condition made even worse by the winter chill, next to Conrad's it seems strong—low and comforting. There's anger there, too. Not at him. At me. The secret of my fire is out now.

It's convenient for both parties that we're ready to leave, then.

There's a silence, a pause in their conversation. I imagine they're embracing, like mother and son. My heart wells in two parts, with grief and fury.

I wish it was true. I wish the lies weren't what they are. I wish Engelberta wasn't the way she is, and somehow it could all be real and good. For Conrad — so he could be truly happy, and not live a lie. He speaks up again.

"And..." he begins, in a whisper. "She... said something stupid. It made me so angry."

"What did she say?"

"That you... I don't believe it, and I didn't, not for one second, I promise..." he trails off, and takes a shaking breath. "That you stole me from my mother, in exchange for her life."

Engelberta is silent. Conrad is quick to fill the lull.

"Don't worry. I know it can't be true, I—"

"You're a good child," she soothes. "You see the lies from truth —the Oakfather wills it. You know in your heart I would never do that to you."

Again, a silence permeates the space, and all I hear are Conrad's quiet sniffles. Engelberta speaks again, unexpectedly. Her voice is like sharp stone.

"I think, perhaps, you should go and fetch Kestra."

I start in the stairwell, hitting my knee against a step. Everything jolts at once and my body is electric, springing down the stairs; I have to run now; *what did I expect from her but this—*

"Kestra." Engelberta's voice echoes. I turn back. Her silhouette is rooted at the top of the stairwell, blocking out what little light there was.

Something about her freezes me in place. A pinch of it is fear, yes, but there's also rage—something deep and vengeful lies inside me. She wants people like me destroyed, before we even do anything wrong. She wants to lie to Conrad for the rest of his life. She wants to kill my family. *My home.*

"Stay." she commands, and I do. Not because I'm listening to her, but because I am listening to myself. Nothing else matters.

She will see that I *know* what she's done.

"I don't want to do this, Kestra." she says.

My stomach coils in on itself in disgust. "Would you say that of *every* terrible thing you've done?"

"*You* cannot speak of terrible things." she bites back. "You weave fire like thread, the element of Death. You are a destroyer, even after being taught that it is wrong. Do you not understand the harm you do?"

Sparks are flying within me; pressure builds painfully in my chest. *I've done nothing wrong—*

My burning home flashes before me. I shake it from my mind, and let myself stand in this moment, eyes alight with hatred.

"The harm that I've done pales next to all that you've destroyed." I growl.

She just stares, eyes cold as a grave.

"There comes a point where every person chooses which side they fight for," she murmurs. "Life or Death. I would ask which side you favour, but it seems you have already chosen."

There's a pause. It lasts too long. *Something's wrong.*

I turn like a terrified animal and see them approaching: vines, big and small, creeping up the stairway behind me. Engelberta's hand twitches and they quicken, ready to curl around me and suck the air from my bones. Buzzing sickness consumes my insides.

I have to run. *There is no running.*

I have to fight, then. I have to do something.

My fire, bright and furious, burns through my heart. *She says I am a destroyer. In this moment, may she be proven right.*

131

My palms were warm with sweat long before this. Flames spring from them just as easily; she flinches minutely. With all my strength, I let the jets of fire grow, spewing their terror upon the stairway.

To my relief, a roiling wall of flame bellows up between us—I can barely see her expression through the dancing light. Behind her, the wood floor begins to catch in the spray of sparks. If no one stops it, the room will be consumed by my fire.

I rip my gaze away. There's no time to lose—I produce enough ribbons of twisting fire to curtail the vines and start dashing down the stairs.

I come to the doorway, frenzied. *Where do I go? What do I do now? Should I find Renate? Should I—*

Before I can begin to decide, a falcon flies down out of the window to Engelberta's room, lands in front of me, and blurs into the shape of Conrad.

"Stop!" he screams, tears struggling to escape his straining face.

"She'll kill me," I breathe, moving past him, "get out of the way. *Please.*"

He stops me forcefully, but I can feel the tremors running through his muscles; there are sobs in him that want to get out. "You can't leave." he rasps. "The Oakfather doesn't will it—you're *sinning—*"

I take a deep breath and lean into him, scrounging for one final hug from my friend, as twisted as it may be.

I've already made my decision.

"If my choice is to be a sinner or die," I begin, "then I have no choice but to sin."

With that, my palms, which still embrace him, burn hot. He yelps and loosens his grip.

I run. Without a second thought, I run. Feet heavy against the sanctuary's frosted grass, I bolt for the edge of it, ready to dive into the forest. The roots of the trees I run past reach out for me, and the earth rises around me like a wall—I glance behind me and see Conrad doing it all, arms outstretched. Behind him lies the church, illuminated from the inside like a flaming beacon. A silhouette appears from the downstairs archway. My heart jolts again.

She's here for me. Didn't even bother to put the fire out.

The earth walls are rising around me. I should shapechange; I should escape across the skies. But that peace I need is nowhere within me right now—I couldn't picture the eagle if I tried.

"Stop, Conrad!" I yell out in futility, "Please, I—"

The walls keep rising.

I point at Conrad. Time seems to slow. *I can't do this. I have to do this. I—*

A sizzling roar screams through the air as a bolt of fire propels itself from my hand.

I hear a scream behind me; it's Conrad's, I know it.

My heart crumples like a piece of torn, burning parchment, but I scramble over one of the lower walls without hesitation. I run on, away from the sanctuary and the church, through the trees; over rocks and moss I flee, bathed in the darkness of the shadows that used to terrify me. All I know is the chase; the feeling of running. The wind isn't singing now; it's screaming past, and it sounds like Conrad.

. . .

When I finally stop, and the dawn is breaking solemnly into the cold clearing I've collapsed in, there is only one thought running through my head.

What have I done?

III: Firestorm

III: FIRESTORM

16

CRYSTALS OF ICE blur across my freezing skin.

I am numb; the fear is there, but it's far away, like someone calling from the other side of a mountain. White dawn stretches into the clearing.

It's cold here. My mind knows it, but my body does not shiver.

Despite the feeling of a gaping hole in my chest, the frenzied night has given way to hollow calm. Here, it is silent—save the blue song of the breeze through leafless trees, and the intermittent snuffling of animals burrowing into their dens.

I am at peace. Numb and empty, but at peace.

I imagine the eagle. After a moment, it arrives in my mind. Time becomes strange, but I don't notice the difference; the world around me is already coldly distant. Soon, I am gone from the clearing and only the eagle remains.

. . .

My flight over Duskwood is dulled by numbness, but as the ribbons of frosty air fly past my feathered face, I begin to feel. Not excitement, or elation, but as though I'm kindling, soon to burn away. A fiery sensation is eating at my chest.

I didn't decide which way to fly, but I find I've been going northwards.

Why not south, to the Spires? Renate has probably already gone that way, though I can't be sure. She's ready to leave. She *must* leave, with or without me. They'll be watching her even more carefully than before.

My heart aches, and I remember her hand in mine. *She won't go,* a part of me says. *Not without you.*

Caught in between the two images—her staying; her leaving— my stomach shivers.

I have no idea what she'll do.

What have Conrad and Engelberta said about me by now? That I'm dangerous, rampaged then stole away, and I must be hunted down? Or perhaps rather that I'm a cowardly sinner, who'll die in the clutches of a Duskwood I barely survived alone?

I'm different now, though—stronger. I can't forget that, even if I feel powerless.

I'm heading north. *To Hanshen? No, but I...*

It feels as though a hand, spectral and blue as the cold of the morning, is pulling me there—a stupid thought. It's my own hand.

The wind lessens again my feathers as I slow, preparing to land. I have to stop and think; it's all too confusing. There are so many things pulling at my heart.

I transform as soon as I touch the ground, finding my human body again. I pull my cloak around me, huddling into it.

An Oak tree arches over me, leafless. Frost is thin on the ground. Despite it, I sit, and place my hand to the cold grass. Beneath it, the earth is hard and freezing, like a corpse.

I breathe. *What should I do? Which choice should I make?*

I know one thing—I cannot stay here. Now is the time to decide. Silence shrouds me, making room for the buzzing chaos of my head to expand, a bloated weight upon my shoulders.

But then there's a thrumming, fainter than the movement of an ant—I feel it in my bones, in my fingers. I stretch my palm against the earth, curious...

Then there's nothing. A cold wind blows limply through the trees. I sigh and let myself relax, staring up at the tree with my hand on the ground.

Then, again, there's something.

It's like the first time I touched the earth and knew it was alive —really alive, just like me.

There. I focus in on it.

It flows through me like a landslide.

A heartbeat, warm and rolling and deep. A moment ago I was hollow—now my being is filled with gentle comfort. It's like an embrace. Like being in Renate's arms, or tucked in bed listening to one of Florian's stories. Soon I feel like a lantern, softly glowing in the snow of the dawn.

The Oak tree stretches up above me, silent. *Is this the Oakfather, creating this warmth?* I'd never properly considered the origins of it all.

A question that sat often at the borders of my mind repeats itself: *if I can create fire, but he abhors it, how can the power come from him?*

I don't know. It's all too complicated—this god, that god.

Rhene didn't smite me for leaving the Path, the Oakfather hasn't relinquished my powers for leaving the church.

There is only one constant. The only thing I can seem to truly rely on is myself.

But then again, this is real. This subtle, rolling heartbeat, locked deep beneath the earth. Duskwood's roots thrum with something real and precious—perhaps the entire world does.

Oh, I would love to see the whole world.

I can see them like they're on the horizon—the Spires, sharp mountaintops protruding from the ground like the discarded swords of giants; then over hills and fields beyond, green and vast, and the smoking mass of Brennof beyond that, caught in my mind's eye...

Then the cities. The bright cities beyond the Hallesee, sparkling with sunlight from a dream.

I am sure of one thing now. Bathing this earth with blood will not heal it. Whether it's Rhene's, or the Oakfather's, or someone else's entirely, it has a heartbeat. Like us, it is alive. I feel its soul in the wind and the rustling of the leaves; in the rough warmth of tree bark, and in the quiet songs of the denizens that know it well, better even than those at the sanctuary.

I feel it now. I am stiller than I've ever been. All I want is to know this place, to understand it better than through some distant explanation of a god.

Without thinking, I rise and step forward, removing my hand from the earth. I can still feel its heartbeat in the air, and through my feet. I reach out for the Oak, expecting cold winter bark... but it's *warm*. Like a creature with a voice, it hums to me, moving in and out of focus.

Plants speak in pictures, Otto said. I never understood

entirely, always struggling to see anything. Now I understand. It's more like music.

The oak's warm thrum is comforting—there's a hope to it. I can't explain it, but it's right there in front of me, undeniable and bright. A joy rushes to my chest, lighter than the wind. It's wonderful; *it's alive.*

Why steal this from people who could learn?

I know they could, if they felt it too. The world is alive like them. The oak's gentle hum rises warmly against my hand, like a chorus.

Yes.

It all comes to me; this is the crucial, echoing moment after an argument, the one where you realise exactly what you should have said.

People *can* learn. They have to be able to.

Hanshen—my family—are no exception. The church has everything: plentiful food, knowledge of Duskwood, and most importantly, a love of it. They've had the tools this whole time, but have only used them to erase.

I know what has to be done. I can't stand by. I have to talk to them. *Otto, Engelberta, Conrad. Ari, Ilse, Leot. Matthias. Folkera. Everyone else.* Even if I die trying, I have to change their minds.

Florian's warm chuckle floats into my mind, and for the first time in a long time, I can picture Liesl's rare little smile. I have to keep my family's blood unspilled, even if Hanshen thought I'd be better off dead.

They didn't understand before. Neither did I. Now I have knowledge—I can begin to explain, at least. And even if they don't try to understand, they're people. Though a simmering resentment still twists in some part of me, it's true. That truth is deeper than my deepest fire, the one I try to keep down, enclosed in the lattice of my fingers.

I can't let them all be murdered. I can't let the people I love and have trained with stain their hands either.

I remove my hand from the oak's bark. My other one is warm. It's flickering with gentle flame, unprovoked by any conscious thought. My rage is the colour of fire, but so too, it seems, is my joy. Perhaps, now, even my peace can be a candle.

I'll use it. Not to destroy—Engelberta's furious voice rings in my head—but to protect. My greatest strength; the thing that is part of me, whether I like it or not: *fire.* But I have to be better. Despite being one with my decision, I have to steel myself. Conrad's echoing scream won't leave me.

I won't let that happen again.

So as the dawn breaks into late morning, I allow myself this little time to practise. It's not much, but it could make the difference.

A cluster of great rocks lies opposite the oaks, spread out in the frosted grass like huge grey gems. Icicles hang like windchimes from trees; my breath freezes the air. Again, I should feel cold, but there's flame beneath my skin.

When I begin, I soon feel like I'm pushing through the heat of Summer. Winter sparkles frostily around me and I set it all adrift. I move like I'm dancing; I'm Renate, moving watery gems with precision, down to the smallest part. I imagine her, and fire pours from my hands—then I stop it; I twist it and control it like it's a grass snake, a rope of flame under my command.

I throw it too, again and again. *Panic will not take me like it did last night.* I choose a rock, then hurl my flames. The globules of fire are great and small—I'm experimenting, controlling everything about them. After each throw, the faint scorch marks are exactly where I planned for them to be. *Control.* A joy rises in my chest again, tinged with bubbling nervousness. *I will choose whether to hit or not. I will choose.*

Afternoon wakes itself, and I am unbearably warm in the pressing cold. My veins sing with the afterburn of fire, and my mouth is drier than dust. Nevertheless, it was the most natural thing. A dance. I could hear the music of Duskwood humming in time with my simmering blood.

My mind pricks at itself. *Even so, I should go now.* I don't know when they'll arrive—whether they're travelling on foot or as birds, or any manner of other creature. *I need to start moving.* My body fights the idea; tendrils of anxiety begin to curl against my ribs. I throw it aside. My body is wrong. My soul is alight. The eagle comes to me in an instant, painted white like snow, and the song of Duskwood's roots transforms the blissful song of the wind.

I am a lightning bolt, crackling straight into the North. I sweep forward like an arrow. The truth is lodged deep inside my feathered chest.

This was never really a choice. She told me to choose, having already designated me as Death.

It's not true. I stand with Life—I will protect it all.

17

LIKE A SHIVERING BLANKET, evening is finally folding over Duskwood. A faint plume of smoke drifts from the trees below. It's been a long flight.

I land far away, perched high up in the lattice of leafless branches. My chest is shaking inside. The questions have started again, running like wild animals through my head: *will Renate be here? Did we both make the same choice? Does Engelberta already know I'm here?*

I've been searching for her since I ran—the green eyed, grey feathered bird that haunted me before I knew her. Rigid, I seek with my eagle's eyes towards the source of the smoke. Dusk is cloaking the forest, but I feel as though I can see everything perfectly. If there weren't trees, the view would go on for miles.

Through the trees, I glimpse the light of a small fire. Figures move around it, and clumps of shadow which must be tents break the rolling ground. Without much thought, I make myself smaller

—I shapechange, faster than I ever have before. I see Renate's bluejay, right there in my mind. I become it. If she sees me, she'll know. She has to.

If she's even there.

I approach, hiding in the shadows of high tree branches. I see them all bustling with provisions, or sitting by the solitary fire. Otto's cooking, with its wonderful, warm scent, drifts up from a pot. Some of them sit around it. There's no chatter, though. It's too solemn.

I count heads. I can't help but notice Ilse, staring off into the dusk. There's Leot, too, running his fingers nervously through the strands of his hair, and Ari, gazing quietly into the fire.

No Engelberta. No Conrad.

The image of him in one of the tents, helping her into a coughing, fitful sleep flits in and out of my mind. My heart wrings itself painfully. Perhaps it's her, helping him with whatever wound I inflicted him with in my frenzy. I rip my thoughts from it. *It hurts. It all hurts.*

Then I see Renate. I know her by just her gait, smooth and quietly purposeful. It's like I haven't seen her for weeks, even though yesterday evening I was lying in her arms. It all seems so far away now. Her hair grew again with the winter—I hadn't noticed until spending time away from her. Now it almost brushes her shoulders. When Spring comes around, she'll shear it all off again, I'm sure of it. She always does. Her eyes are dark and watchful and her expression's blank, like a locked box. Even I can't tell what she's really feeling—though it might just be our distance from each other.

She's walking to the edge of the encampment, ignoring Otto's call to join them at the fire. Despite the cold, when she stops, she's statuesque, standing still against a nearby tree trunk.

Perfect.

I dislodge a small twig from the branch I'm on and carry it in my talons. Like a blue shadow, I glide over the encampment, timing my drop...

I release the twig, and it bounces off her head. She looks up.

I've landed on a branch above her. Her acknowledgement, though unknowing, opens the gates for relief to flood through my tense chest. In a burst of stupid confidence, I make a hushed squawking sound.

Something flickers in her expression. Her mouth twitches. She glances back to the encampment, then up at me. Then she begins to wander farther away from the others, melting slowly into the darkening forest. As soon as she's far enough away, her form folds into a flurry of feathers, revealing a twin bluejay.

She flits away and I follow her. It's comforting, after everything, to be guided.

We stand in a frost-laced clearing.

"Finally." Renate says. "I was expecting you."

My heart swells, and I can't do anything but draw her in for a hug—I cling to her like my life depends on it, and she doesn't pull away.

So she knew me better than I knew myself.

To her, it was simple: of course I wouldn't be able to leave, knowing that my home would be destroyed. She heard it in my pauses as we talked of leaving; she saw it in my scattered, blank expressions. It never occurred to me that she had learnt to read me, too—though perhaps I'm more of an open book.

"Of course you were," I breathe.

I proceed to explain the situation—the things I found in Engelberta's rooms, the truth about Conrad's origins, and how they both found out. Her expression doesn't flicker. She's been sceptical this whole time; despite the wonder of the teachings and the friendship, she saw everything as it was. The things left unsaid spoke louder than any teaching.

"Conrad's real mother," I say, "She might be out there somewhere, but he'll never get to see her again. It's like he doesn't even believe she exists."

My heart skips a beat. In Renate's presence, the memory of his scream had dulled itself. As it echoes in my head again, I wince.

"How is he? I think... I..."

She holds me close, and lets us sit in the lull.

"Nothing that won't heal." she murmurs. "You just about missed his eye."

A straining, hot numbness aches through me. The blood is rushing to my head; it's like I'm in a horrible, distant dream... Then I rein myself in. It hurts. *But it's done. I'll apologise when— When—*

I don't know when. Not now. The only opportunity would be during the fighting. An impossible task—though this entire gambit seems impossible, so who truly knows?

"When will the attack begin?"

"Tomorrow morning."

Silence eats the clearing. Our warm heartbeats are the only sensation outside of the barren cold.

I look into Renate's face. The words are sticking in my throat.

I gulp. She presses her hand against my heart and feels the quick beat.

"Will you help me?" I croak.

She laughs. She always laughs at the strangest times. She takes me by the back of my head, pressing our foreheads together. We stand there, one, in the darkening Duskwood.

"Always." she whispers.

18

WHAT LITTLE SLEEP I can snatch, I grab with both hands.

In my dreams, a burning Hanshen rises before me. I bat it away with all my might.

I won't let it happen. I'll control myself. I'll stop everything.

The night, despite its coldness, was kind. Renate smuggled me a blanket or two, and food, so I didn't have to hunt. I curled up in a rocky hollow and let my skin warm itself, to fill whatever heat I needed in excess of the blankets. I don't need to start fires, it seems. I can just push myself right to the brink of flame; warm hands, warm arms, warm face—as though the blood's rushing to all of them at once, simmering like a hearty soup.

Last night, we planned.

Renate tells me that after I ran, she tested the waters with Ilse. As they talked, it wasn't long until Renate felt safe asking for help from all three of them: Ilse, Ari and Leot. There's doubt churning horribly inside them, as it did in us. We are not Conrad, or the older druids—Engelberta's claws haven't been in us for long enough. Even if she sees us as malleable children, she cannot change us enough to make us kill innocents.

Renate says she and the others will divert as many of the druids from harming the villagers as she can. They'll fight, if necessary, differentiating themselves by throwing off their cloaks.

I'm ready to fight too, though I'll make sure to scare and distract rather than burn flesh. I don't know if I could handle doing that again.

We also discussed whether I should warn the village.

I can't, was my first thought. *They'll have harpoons in me before I can utter one word.*

Then Florian's stories floated back into my head, though, wondrous and warm. I remember how I whispered to him about the shipwreck in Chapel, knowing that no one but him would believe me. So I said I'd ask him. I can't picture his reaction, seeing me out of nowhere after two years—but no matter what he might do, I have to at least try to warn him.

Light is barely peeking through the trees, bouncing off whatever crystals of frost it can find. I rise without thought—I must be first, no matter what, and I can't be far from Hanshen now.

I become an eagle, sharp-eyed and swift winged. Again, I head north like something's pulling me there. The tree-lattices swirl beneath me, coming and going faster than ocean waves.

I see it up ahead. I see the lights. In the morning hours, the fishermen begin their preparations. As a small child, sometimes, I would sneak out and watch, only to be coaxed by Florian into going home, lest Mother see the hint of curiosity in me and seek to stamp it out.

He was kind. He protected me in the only way he could—he fed me what I loved, stories, but he also tried to shield me from the punishments he knew would come if I kept acting the way I did. My heart is in my throat. *He has to believe me when I speak to him, he...*

I don't even know what he looks like anymore. He's probably much taller; he might have even grown a beard. Perhaps I won't be able to recognise him at all.

Even so, I can see his gait in my mind, as distinct as Renate's.

Yes, there it is too—the cheerful twist of his smile, as clear as if he's before me.

Hanshen sprawls out beneath me like a labyrinth, much bigger than it ever was. Our fields—their fields—are vaster than ever. I could have sworn to Rhene that the space bounded by Duskwood was never that large. Engelberta's wrathful eyes enter my mind. *Ah, yes. They began cutting down the trees—burning some, even, for land space. I* wonder how many children have been born since I left; I wonder how many may be born yet. Plentiful recruits, to take and become druids.

The more I think about it, the more it enrages me. *Why only children? Can all of Hanshen not eventually learn our ways?*

Both sides have tried to kill me. I was too strange for Hanshen; I was too strange for the Church. They both need someone strange to look at, then. To tell them a hard truth.

If I run now, neither of them will ever learn.

One moment I'm soaring, studying the changing form of my once-home like it's one of Conrad's sketches. Then, with my eagle eyes, I see someone with a familiar gait, alone, walking down to shore.

I glide in, waiting for him to step behind the tall rock cliff that hides part of the shore from the village. *It's now or never.* I swoop, heart racing, and in my anxious wobbling, I barely miss his shoulder with my talons.

Florian jumps, and yells; in these hazy seeds of dawn, it must seem like I'm a dark spirit from Duskwood, coming down to attack him. Immediately, I fold my form up into itself.

With my new eyes, I immediately realise it is much darker than I thought it was. Without delay, I snap my fingers and let a flame come alight within my hand, hoping to whichever god is real that we really are alone.

In the light of the flame, his eyes are bright with terror. It strikes me cold to my core. *What did I expect?* He's already readied himself, muscles taut, facing me. I see the sudden glint of a dagger in his hand. His face hasn't changed much; it's a little more worn, but I'm sure I could say the same for mine. His hair has grown— now he wears it tied back from his face. And he's definitely taller. I have to look up to see him properly.

Thanks to the fire, my face too is illuminated. At the resultant change in his expression, my terror vanishes in almost an instant, and air enters my lungs again.

"Is this real?" he croaks, voice much deeper than the time we last spoke. He doesn't move an inch. He only stares, transfixed, as though he's scared to blink.

I'm the one to step forward. I don't know what to say. My heart is welling up in my throat; if I speak I might start crying and never stop.

I embrace him as best I can, hands shaking. At the knowledge that I'm real, Florian's demeanour shifts. He pulls his arms around me, though I feel the tense movement of his neck as he looks around in vain for anyone that might have seen me. Soon, he settles.

"Kestra," he whispers. "You're alive."

"Mostly thanks to you." I say into his chest, breathing in the strange, stable scent of the home that abandoned me.

It's strange, how much I still care about them all.

I soon break out of the hug. It hurts to do it, but my heartbeat won't slow down. *They're coming, I know it. We have to do something. Now.*

"I'm sorry to do this," I say, "but we don't have time."

"What do you mean?"

"You saw what I can do." I point with my other hand to the fire, reignited in my hand. "The Speaker was right... In a way. There are people like me in the South. Witches, I suppose, but not really. They're kind... Well, I thought they were—they love the wood, and work in harmony with it, but..." I pause for breath, and my thoughts buzz in the empty space. *How do I explain this without painting them as monsters?* They're not, I know it; Engelberta is misguided and angry and desperate. We have some of the younger druids on our side, but the older druids would do anything for her.

"Hanshen is in danger. Engelberta—she leads the druids, and she's angry. She's dangerous."

He's silent, taking it in. I continue:

"You've been eating into Duskwood and burning the wood of the trees you don't need. What happened to following the Path?"

The Path was impossible for me to follow, but it seems that it had, in some way, been keeping Hanshen safe.

Florian wears an expression of intense confusion. For me,

though, he sees my panicked eyes and pushes it aside; I watch it happen. Gratitude flows through me like a wave.

"Not long after you ran," he explains, "the Speaker died."

A cold shock folds over me. I don't know why; it was coming. He was the oldest man I'd ever seen.

Florian continues:

"He had no living sons—they'd all died at sea. Things became chaotic—no one knew who should replace him. The strongest men in the village had been sent after you and never returned, so they couldn't fill the space he left. None of us could honestly claim to hear Rhene's commands, or even wanted the burden of living up in that draughty chapel."

At the mention of the dead fishermen, he glances at the flame in my hand. I shake my head. *I didn't kill them.* Vines wrapped their corpses—then there was only the haunting song of a grey bird.

"Anyway, because Mother repented so completely after everything that happened with you, our family wasn't completely shunned. At a village meeting, amongst all the squabbling, I suggested we vote on the important things, instead of putting the burden of being Speaker on one person. The other men laughed a little at first. Once they saw I was serious, though, they had enough respect for me to entertain it—though not for long, they warned. It would never work.

"But after a few months working that way, things settled down; we all got into the rhythm of it, and had a prosperous year of fishing and a great harvest, better than we've had in living memory. One thing led to another, and now... Well, without the Speaker's sermons, the atmosphere around the Path relaxed a little. What if we extended it, some thought, to make more room for fields? How could Rhene see that as bad, if it increased the number of his followers?"

It's a lot to take in. My head is full of it, imagining the time passing in this place. *So much change. Although...*

"Do the women get to vote?" I blurt out.

He glances guiltily away.

"Not yet," he says, "but—"

"If we don't all die, that has to change."

I glance up at the lightening sky. *There's no more time.*

I turn and prepare to shapechange again.

"Help them escape along the shore to the West," I call back to him, "tell them witches are coming, from beyond the Path. I hope that scares them enough to go with you. Also, look out for help from those of us that are against this—we'll throw off our cloaks to make it clear."

"Alright," he breathes, and his boots begin to thud away on the sand.

"And, Florian?" I shout back. "Remember this, if they ask: I'll be fighting for them all, even if some of them wouldn't fight for me."

Then I am an eagle, and the sea salt wind is singing past me as I fly back over Hanshen through the breaking dawn.

convincing more of the other druids that this is wrong, away from Engelberta. Or, at worst, knocking them unconscious, or even...

Fresh shouts and screams of fear sound from behind me—my flame wall has burned out: the village sees it all. Their fabled witches, approaching like hungry beasts from the forest. I only hope most of the residents are going or already gone.

My eyes remain fixed on the group moving towards me. I hold my warm palms up, ready. Engelberta's stare does not leave me.

One step, two steps, three steps. Closer now.

My hands flare and become beacons of roiling flame. There's a beat of hesitation in some of the remaining druids' movements, cautious against something new and unknown. Yet Engelberta doesn't seem to react; she only marches forward, eyes bright green with growing hatred.

I'm ready. Whatever comes next will come.

Eyes never leaving mine, she continues to advance.

Then she flicks her hand in command, and they fold into themselves in an instant—a flurry of birds rises in the air. They soar right over me, leaving me facing a bare field.

In a heartbeat, I turn and run back through the village gate. The druids' silhouettes streak ahead, coming down in too many places to count. I bolt through the streets, scouring every inch for any villager that might be left behind.

The path is hard with frosted mud; my feet slam like drums in a tortured beat. A cacophony of cracking roars around me; timber is breaking, splintering like Engelberta's voice in a rage. Screams continue to ring out in the distance. *Is it those who are running or people getting hurt?*

A brown-cloaked figure flicks into my vision—they raise their hands and great vines and heaving mounds of earth stab into the sky like lightning from the ground. A house is cracked in two, crumbling in the maw of the earth that eats it.

At the sight of me, the druid runs into a side street. I follow.

We stand between two houses. At my back, I hear the heavy rumble of an earth wall emerging from the ground, cutting off my escape.

No running now.

It's all second nature at this point—my heart pounds and fire erupts from my hands; amidst the relative silence of the alley, it's the only sound, roaring like a wild beast.

The druid begins to bring up another wall between us, as though they've reconsidered fighting me.

I begin to turn away. *Fine. I have people to save.* But then I catch the shadow of another person, cowering behind them, all hunched over. If I leave now, that person is dead.

I won't let this happen. I leap up onto the wall as it rises, my flaming hands scorching the fresh earth.

"Don't!" I shout, jumping down between the two figures. In the proximity and light, I see their faces clearly, illuminated by my desperate fire.

The cowering figure is an old man. His eyes are milky with blindness, but his face is contorted with terrified confusion.

The druid is Conrad.

A raw patch of scarring lies on his left cheekbone, very close to his eye. I want to look away, to run; I feel sick, like there are eels churning in my stomach—

But he's already jumping back, hood slipping from his head. There's a look of desperate agony twisting his face.

"Conrad!" I shout. "Do you really want to make my village bleed like this?"

Vines spring from the earth, grabbing for the old man and I. Panting, I drag him out of the way with one hand, burning what attacks I can with the other.

"Conrad!"

Vines spring at me again. I keep pulling the old man back; we're slowly retreating down the alley.

"Please! Listen to me!"

The barrage continues. I dart and dodge at best I can given my burden. *It's working.* Earth and vine wilt alike under my fiery hands—but I'm so warm, I need to take a breath, *there's no time*—

After shouting enough times for the old man to go, he's started scrambling on his own towards the end of the alley. I shield his escape. Conrad's biting vines chase like snakes, but I don't stop, throwing balls of flame to nullify them, wincing every so often when I hear them sizzle.

But I hit where I wanted. I can do this.

The old man's shadow has vanished from the end of the street. I only hope whichever god cares about any of this will let him escape the other druids.

I grant myself one deep breath of relief, and stare back at Conrad. He's boxed himself in with his own wall; in the chaos, we've switched places in the alley. Like me, his breaths are rapid. His face is contorted in desperation. I step forward.

"Stay away!" he shouts.

I don't stop. *I can't.*

"I want to apologise!" I yell back, throat hoarse, eyes pricking with my own smoke. "Please!"

He holds his hand out like he's about to unleash another round of attacks. I see its tremors, though. My hands are shaking too.

We're about two metres from each other. He hasn't moved to do anything. He just stares at the fire in my hands.

I look to him, and then the fire. I extinguish it.

"Please listen," I stutter, "I'm sorry. I'm so sorry. For all of it, I'm sorry. For hurting you like that—for telling you the truth the way I did."

"You can't keep calling it the truth," he hisses, voice cracking like he's staring down a cliff edge. "*Stop it.*"

I gesture around. Rumbling floats across the air from other parts of Hanshen. The distant screams have already died on the wind.

"Would someone who wants the best for you make you do this?"

Silence. His hand trembles.

"I know," I coax, still trying to catch my breath, "it's difficult to admit that the one who raised you isn't good."

My mother's image flashes through my mind. Terror and hatred burn together in her eyes, and the echoing, damp stone of the Hold rings like death in my bones.

"You could have another one, though," I whisper desperately. "A mother, out there somewhere."

He stares, eyes wet. I try again. *All I have is the truth.*

"We're children, Conrad. No one should be making us kill. It's not right. Deep down, you know that."

His hand drops to his side and he stands immobile, scarred face staring blankly down at the ruined path. I edge forward, careful not to do anything rash despite the awful aching in my chest.

Somehow, I need to make him see.

"Renate and I care about you." I say, throat thick with

heartache, "I missed you. It destroyed me not knowing how badly I'd hurt you."

The earth is wet with tears, dripping from his downturned face to the path.

"Can I...?" I begin, but he's already grabbed on to me like his life depends on it. I tense at first, prepared for a vine to slither around my neck.

It never comes.

Exhausted, I relax into his unexpected hug. Tears are welling up in my own eyes, blurring the world around me. My heart is bleeding—*or is it healing? Maybe that hurts just as much.*

"I need to speak to her," Conrad croaks. "We need to talk."

20

HE LEAVES with a measure of determination in his steps, but I see he's still fragile. Anyone would be, with their world turned upside down like that. My heart still aches—with fear for him, and in the aftershock of his forgiveness.

It won't help for me to be there, enraging Engelberta, so I walk in the opposite direction—I need to find Renate. I only hope her blood doesn't stain the sand already.

My pace quickens to a run. Houses creak like blown trees in a raging wind; vines crawl the streets in place of people. I see various cloaks of brown, whose gazes I try to slip past, but very few villagers.

I reach the northern edge of Hanshen and absorb a view of the shore from my position, sandwiched into a side-street. Chaos pours west. I can't make it all out.

That's where I need to go, to make sure they're all safe—

Otto's face flashes past my hiding place, framed in the hood of his cloak. He's running straight at someone.

I don't see who his target is, but I hear a high-pitched scream. The sound of it jolts me out onto the main street. Dual thoughts drive themselves into my skull:

How could Otto fall this low?

I have to help.

He's grabbed the wrist of a girl—she has brown hair, and is pale, quite short—

Liesl! I rush out at him, forgetting all resignations I might have had about attacking Otto. It's strange—Liesl was always a shadow in my life, but now that she's in danger, my rage is burning hot as ever.

"Do not fear!" he says, trying to calm her. "We are saving you from here, to learn the right ways!"

Vines have begun to sprout from the ground around her terrified form. My heart is jolting in my dry mouth. His hand remains like a clamp around her small wrist, and his voice grows louder and more desperate every second, as though the more he shouts the more it will placate her.

It does the exact opposite.

A piercing scream resounds like it's coming from everywhere at once. There's a flash of light; the air crashes and splits like cracked glass. *Lightning.* Coming not from the sky but from... *Liesl?*

Wind is swirling across the seafront, working in forceful tendrils into a whirlwind around them. It pushes me back. I try to split the current, to move it away. It takes more strength than I've ever had to use to manipulate air.

After a handful of seconds, the wind clears. There lies Otto, traces of smoke rising from his right arm. Around it, his robe and cloak are burnt to cinders.

Liesl stands rigid, slowly stumbling back from him.

"Liesl!" I shout. She looks at me, eyes widening further. "There's no time to talk!" I continue. "Join the others on the western shore!"

If you can help, please do, I want to say, but the shock in her blank face is haunting.

This was the first time that has happened to her.

What it was, exactly, I don't know. *Air, earth, water, fire... Lightning?* This world of magic must be much broader than Engelberta ever taught us—but what should I have expected other than omissions of the truth?

Liesl stumbles past me. I want to hug her and tell her there's nothing wrong with her, but she goes quickly, like a terrified animal—away in a blink.

Now for Otto. Though he's lying sprawled on the floor, he's still conscious. His arm has been burnt raw; shapes like lightning thread jaggedly across it. As I come to stand over him, he takes a breath to talk. I speak first.

"Stop this, or stay down," I say, hand promptly alight with flame, "and don't try to hurt my sister again."

Defending Liesl. If rage wasn't searing my heart, I might laugh —*I truly am a different person now.*

He raises his left hand in surrender, face slack with burgeoning realisation. Perhaps if he's made to lie there for a while he'll begin to rethink his choices. I turn on my heel and sprint down to the beach.

A blur of villagers, clad in their familiar greys, rushes like a stream of tumbling rocks down the light slope of the beach. Mouth dry, I run past them searching for brown-cloaked druids and finding none. My eye catches a flash of deep green—there they are: Renate, Leot, Ilse. As planned, they've thrown off their sanctuary brown to distinguish themselves from the attackers. As I approach, I see them speaking gently, guiding tentative villagers alongside Florian and some of the other men.

He stands like a leader, I note with a strange pride. Without him vouching for my friends it may have been impossible for us to help.

A couple of brown-cloaked bodies lie a little way away, at the foot of the cliffs. Ari is crouched next to one of them, examining, stony-eyed. I register splatters of blood around the bodies, staining the sand. A sickness creeps into my throat. I can't tell whether they're alive or dead. I suppose that's what Ari is checking for.

I feel sick. *Which would be better for us?*

"Kestra!" Renate shouts. My ears prick at the raw touch of excitement in her voice.

I run over, speeding up again. Her hair is darkly windswept; she's breathing heavily. Though she's bright with the electric tension of battle, there's a blank shock sitting in the pits of her eyes.

"Is everyone alright?" I huff, lungs burning.

For a moment, Renate is silent, breathing in the salt air alongside me. She just stares in her way—not at me, this time, but past me, like she's gazing into nothing.

"I..." she begins. "They wouldn't listen. They got close—close to killing a lot of your people. It was a split second thing."

I've never seen her stammer like this; her words escape her like birds before she can bite down on them.

I understand one thing. The brown cloaked bodies on the ground are not alive.

"I used wind." she says bleakly. "To knock them away, when we were all up there. They fell from the cliff. It was all so fast."

I'm staring at where the two druids fell. Her eyes refuse to touch that space.

"I didn't realise any of this could be made that deadly." she murmurs. The blank shock reveals itself again in her hollow voice. "I guess that's what we were taught it for, after all. To kill these people."

Her eyes lift to the grey clothed villagers that traipse past us.

We continue guiding them. Some eyes lie on us, suspicious and afraid, but with Florian and some of the men in our midst, we are tentatively accepted. The villagers all seem shocked, still, caught in the rushing terror of what they've just escaped.

I can even make out the faraway face of my mother, grey as the morning sky. Her eyes do not leave me, but strangely, I couldn't care less. All I can think of is Renate.

What she did... what she had to do... it swirls in my head, overwhelming as a swarm of shadows—but it must be worse for her. Whenever I glance over at her, it's like I'm watching her pack her feelings into a box, locking them away for later. Some of the men look at her with expressions close to gratitude, though. *She saved their families, and they know it. Good.*

In the tense heaviness of our windswept silence, a rumble groans through the air. A wall of earth, taller than any of the houses that still stand, bursts from the ground within Hanshen.

A jolt strikes me to my core.

Conrad.

I'm already running back up the sandy banks, sand spraying in scattered waves in my wake.

21

THE STREETS ARE SCATTERED with fallen rubble. At the sight of the battle within the village, the others came with me, leaving the villagers to make their way farther along the western shore. Our boots thump haphazardly across mud streets and around debris.

We approach the clamouring chaos at Hanshen's centre.

The newly-risen wall of earth stands tall, until it doesn't. With a crash and a crumble of dirt, it comes down before our eyes, showering us with clods of earth. Beyond it, I glimpse a tall figure, hunched over and coughing, and a smaller one, fallen on the ground, poised as though ready to scramble away. Vines as thick as tree trunks wind up from the ground and hover like the tentacles of some forgotten deep sea beast, ready to suffocate and bludgeon anything that moves. With the figure's coughs, the vines twitch menacingly, ready to strike.

"Engelberta!" I scream. "You don't have to do any of this!"

She glances my way—the others already know what to do. The

moment her pale face turns to mine, Ari's carefully placed blast of air has propelled Conrad's body away, sliding him from his place on the ground to the arms of the group.

He has new bruises, and blood seeping from a cut above his eyebrow onto the raw skin of his new burn scar. Putting all of those things aside, he looks ill. There's a greenness to him, and a blankness in the set of his eyes. Confusion lies awakened in the twist of his sickened face.

She turned on him.

The woman he saw as his mother decided that he could no longer learn.

And what is the punishment for those she deems cannot learn?

Renate, shielded by the others, begins to soothe and clean his wounds with the air's water.

Death is the punishment.

Her eyes are so green—like a forest-brewed poison, fixed on me. I ignite my hand like I'm drawing a sword. This time, she doesn't blink.

My arms shake; the nervous tremors run through me like electricity. I hear her question in my mind; I see her flashing resolve.

At some point, everyone makes their choice: to serve the greater forces of Life or Death. Which will you choose?

Her question was a trap. She is supposed to be Life. And in her eyes, I'm Death. Yet I have taken no life, and she has killed more than I can count. Our positions twist and turn within my mind, reversed.

I will answer her question, destroyer or not.

She is silent, fixing me with a dark glare—a glare so sure that it knows better than a child.

There will be no persuading. I tried, though. That's all I can do.

My hands are trembling—the flame sputters at my fingertips. She approaches. I steel myself. *I am not alone.* I feel their presence behind me—here, together, we can preserve life. *I will not run.* My fire regains its power, bursting in roiling waves like an extension of my arms. I am wreathed in it.

"I choose Life." I mutter. I don't know if she hears it. It won't matter either way.

She rushes forward, vines in tow; I jump back, and right, then left. I singe the vines by my very presence. I jump again, onto one of the vines that's thick enough for human feet, use it as a path and lunge for her, hoping desperately to achieve a non-lethal knockout, like Liesl did against Otto.

A foolish overestimation. She recoils from my blow with the speed of a hummingbird, leaping onto one of her other vines. In that instant, her hands make a violent movement; I'm thrown sideways off the vine by a blast of wind, and I'm falling, falling, *falling—*

Thin arms catch me, saving me from a bruising connection with the ground. I collapse alongside their bearer—Leot. From a distance, Engelberta is coughing as though her lungs are about to come up through her throat. I right myself and suck in whatever desperate breath I can.

Approaching footsteps rush from behind our group, mingling with the sound of Conrad's miserable groans and Renate's attempts to soothe him.

"Others?" I breathe, poised to rush back towards Engelberta.

Leot, immediately up and facing the opposite direction, pats me on the shoulder. "We'll do our best, be they friend or foe," he huffs, "you do yours."

So we part like two birds passing each other in the sky, unerring.

Faster, I tell myself, *while she's still coughing and I have a chance of immobilising her.*

Power simmers beneath her skin, honed by years of practice I do not want to comprehend—but it's all choking in the face of her illness. *Perhaps this is my gift from the Oakfather.*

Before I get to her, she's up again, arms out. The vines come for me as fast as lightning bolts; the earth shifts beneath my feet like it's trying to swallow me up. I jump and dodge again, sight fixed ahead—even if I can't stop her completely, I'll keep her as busy as I can. From the noise behind me, it sounds as though the others already have enough to deal with.

Shouts and rumbling echo through the streets, running thick with the sound of battle. *First, try to make them see,* I pray. *Let them understand there is a better way.*

A clod of earth pushes up from beneath my feet, throwing me upwards. I take a breath, feeling the singing air... then I use it all, twisting my burning hands behind me and propelling myself right at her. Her eyes widen a little. Triumph swells in my chest.

She masters herself; the air hisses to my right.

A shockwave of pain crashes into my jaw. I fall, and the ground meets me as an enemy. I hear a sickening crunch from my left shoulder, but I feel it more. It's screaming, searing like the hottest fire imaginable. A vine with all the force of the strongest fist smashed me out of the air. Blurry-eyed, I gaze at it looming above me. Breath forces itself rapidly in and out of my body. The seconds are slowing. I roll from where I am, anticipating the crashing thump of the vine where I once was.

I have to get up.

But when I try, I can't move.

I twist painfully to the side and see a spreading mass of small green tendrils, slithering like snakes from the ground beneath me.

She's so close to me, controlling them with the jerking movements of her fingers. I struggle, pulling with all my might, but I only have one arm to use. A tickling pressure is sliding over my neck. Breath will soon be gone from me. I'm going to become like them, those dead fishermen with their bloodless faces and contorted expressions, frozen where I am right now—

No. Pressure is building fast, but there is time, if only a second. I just need to go inside. I gaze inwards at the timeless cavern of my mind; I stare into the golden eyes of the eagle. Everything stills. Time becomes strange.

Then it's as easy as blinking.

I open my eyes, and I fly. *I've slipped her net.*

Engelberta's shout of irritation reaches me as I soar up into the sky. The pain in my shoulder has not left me—it hovers like a phantom—but I can fly. This eagle's body is different and somehow unharmed, even if the hurt exists in my mind. Questions pool within me. I throw them aside. *No time to ponder.*

I glide in a semicircle and fix Engelberta with a stare. Then I swoop down like an arrow, talons and beak poised in their deadly sharpness. She reaches for wind, but I can see it already; it's in my feathers. I feel subtle beginnings—strange eddies in the air where there should be none. I avoid them before they truly exist, gliding and rolling in an effortless dance; if nothing else, I know the wind's blissful song. After each attempted blow, my course rights itself, again and again, until I'm so close, only half a second away. I can see her vengeful eyes and her hands and her blood and where it will drip from my talons-

Then there is a familiar, terror inducing roar—as though the sun grew teeth and screamed. Searing pain rips through me. I am burning. *I am burning.* I can smell my own flesh boiling; charred feathers scatter as I'm thrown back by the force of whatever hit me. Then I can't see. All I sensed in that moment was agony, white and red and orange—now there is nothing but the sounds of her hacking coughs and the thick, choking smell of smoke.

The eagle is no more, but I am the eagle.

I'm thinking clearly; I haven't died. I want to scream, but I can't. Everything is dark. *How...?* A moment passes. I sense it coming, then. Time is always strange in the moment when forms change like clothes.

I'm forced to fold up into myself, heaving. Light bursts through my eyelids and the pain in my crushed shoulder twists back into being. The realisation comes like lightning: *she burnt the eagle's body to a crisp, but didn't hurt mine.*

Around me, everything flammable is smouldering. The ground is black with ash. I'm covered in it too. I scramble to my feet, clutching my arm.

Engelberta's hands are simmering. They're a bright, angry red —like they're covered in fresh burns. Her face is blank at first glance—it's as though for her, time has stopped as well. Then the shock turns to something I can only place as agony.

"Do you see?" she screams, gesturing wildly at the smouldering chaos around us. "*That* is what happens!"

Her voice is no longer the bark of that great oak, bending in the wind. It's a river, crashing against rocks that will not move, no matter the effort. Despite her years, she looks like a scared child, made wild by confusion.

She's truly unravelling. She has been this whole time.

"You're wrong." I croak, edging towards her. "You're scared of it. You're scared of me."

She just stares, like I'm not there.

Smoke billows in thick curtains around us. Shouting and rumbling rages in the near-distance.

"When you see it for what it is," I continue, "you can control it as you will." My throat aches with the choking smoke, but I rasp on, trying to get through the blankness of her petrified form. "It's neither good nor bad, just a part of you. It can destroy life, yes, but it can also protect life. You can *decide* what to do with it."

She remains blank, staring at her burnt hands. The beginnings of cough subtly wrack her form. In the relative safety of the lull, I get closer, gazing into her face.

"You have control over this." I insist. She looks down at me, and then away.

"The smoke..." she murmurs. "It suffocated my sibling. And the others. Almost everyone I knew. Too many to count."

Brennof. She's talking about Brennof, I know it. She came from there, from the grey burning factory spires and the dark trading streets. She lost people. She abhors the raging flames that lay at the foot of their suffering.

"We wouldn't let any of that happen," I begin, "this isn't the same—"

"Everyone is the same." she murmurs softly, "But you're too young to understand that."

She coughs again. Now that I'm close to her, I notice a new trace of blood dripping from her mouth.

We're both so tired.

Then her arms are around me, gently, and know she's too weak to fight anymore. She couldn't do a thing to me, not after that painful burst of fire.

She's just an old woman, now. *A mother, about to die.*

Conrad needed a mother, because of her. And, cruelly, she fulfilled that role. *I wanted one too,* I think. *But I could never give myself to her. Not the way I am.*

She's dying. I can feel the rattling of her ribs against mine. Even so, as I did with Conrad, I'm waiting, tense, for a vine to sneak around my neck. I'm ready to transform again, although the thought exhausts me.

Five seconds. Ten seconds. Thirty seconds.

Nothing.

This is it for her.

So I return her embrace, and I mourn what she could have been. *If something had been different, early on.*

I can feel her fading, now. She must know it too. The silence around us is empty.

Then there's a sudden heat. It's not mine.

I can't pull away. Her arms tighten around me.

Something's wrong. I was wrong.

"May the Oakfather forgive us both," she whispers hoarsely, "in our next lives."

Time slows. I struggle with all my might, but a second isn't enough time to do anything. Her skin is brightening like there's something emerging beneath the surface; she simmers with rising flame, burning and burning and *burning*—

Then there's nothing at all.

22

I NEVER THOUGHT I'd die by fire. Especially not by Engelberta's. The look on her face when she first realised that fire had come from her own hands won't leave me, even in the second of my death.

I saw loss there. It was something I don't think I could ever properly understand, even if I had any more time.

My fire doesn't hurt me. Perhaps it's because I don't want it to —I make it, after all. Why shouldn't it follow my rules? Her fire, though—it's the opposite. I saw the state of her hands, red with fresh burns. Her fire hurts everyone, because in her mind, it can do nothing else. It smokes far more than mine ever did, because that is what it did in the town where she was born. People choked on it. It got into their lungs, like it did hers, and killed them slowly. Brennof, painted from Florian's stories, is easy to imagine: great fires roaring in the bellies of blackened factories, paving the streets with ash.

Engelberta's hell.

A flash of oblivion shot through my head before I could feel the heat begin to truly burn.

Time has become strange again. My body knew to transform.

So I'm not dead yet. But I will be, if I don't think fast. The eagle is here, and the cavern of my mind isn't as blank as it once was.

I'm in the secret glade. The eagle's eyes are as golden as ever.

It's not enough. The searing agony of cooking bird flesh returns to me. I blink, trying to shake the sensation from my thoughts.

When I open my eyes, the bird is alight.

Not just alight. This is a different bird.

Its feathers have become a reddish-brown, though its eyes continue to bore into me, the same unerring gold. Fire wreaths it like a roiling cloak, stitched into the fibres of its being. Surface feathers merge into flames, giving the bird a bright silhouette against the dusky forest.

A phoenix.

It's the creature from Roth's sketchbook. I didn't think it was real. Perhaps it isn't—this is my mind, after all, and I've imagined it before. After I saw it, it occasionally took shape in my dreams, in the fires of Hanshen. Never this vividly, though. The thought of that dream sickens me. It has come to pass: Engelberta and I are going up in flames, right at Hanshen's centre.

No. Time is strange. We don't have to be dead. Rather, I don't have to be.

I walk forward, reaching out to the phoenix.

My hand is alight too, and when our flames meet, there is a burst of something bright. It's engulfing us. We burn together, without pain.

Reality shoots back into focus. I can smell the smoke, and

taste it. My arm is aching again, but it's relegated to my mind, as it was before.

The realer sensation is the blissful heat I'm bathed in.

I have wings. I have feathers. I'm a phoenix, set alight.

Engelberta's arms have slipped from me and I am flying once again. Everything is in bright focus. The heat is wonderful—it frees me. It's exploding around us, soothing my lighted feathers like a warm bath.

Then I hear her screams.

When the blast clears, I glimpse her from the sky. Parts of her skin are a terrible red, and her hands are almost black. Blood continues to pour from her mouth at every shaking cough. Small fires burn around us, on parts of houses that haven't been completely blackened or eviscerated. The earth is scorched a dark, dying colour, like Death itself.

And they're all watching us. I see their faces, even at this distance, with my new, flaming eyes. *Renate. Conrad. Ari. Leot. Ilse.* Even Otto has managed to limp up from where he lay. Folkera and Matthias watch us too, though it seems the others have had to restrain them.

Many things lie in their expressions. Terror, that familiar bright-eyed beast, is there, but there's an awe to it, too. I imagine how I must look, cloaked in fiery radiance. Bright-winged and sharp-beaked, golden eyes piercing them.

I'm thankful for whatever it was that brought me that phoenix, even if it was just my own desperate mind. But now I must be myself.

I land, keeping a safe distance from Engelberta. She can't stop coughing; it sounds like her lungs are truly about to be wrenched from her chest. Tear tracks run in thin lines through the soot on her burnt face. I fold back into myself—immediately, a jolt of pain rolls through me from my shoulder.

It's enough to knock me down. I try to prop myself up, shaken by heaving breaths, expecting more resistance—*from her, or from the others, or—*

The swooping beat of wings catches my ears. From my place on the ground, I twist my head round, staring up at the source of the noise.

His antlered, winged silhouette sits dark against the morning sky, though his eyes almost glow in their amber way. Wind-ruffled hair pours down his shoulders.

Veiled shock has crept across his face. He lands, and a silence sweeps over us again.

"Roth." I blurt. He glances over at me.

His eyes are wet. A deep sadness is woven into the set of his dark features, and I don't know what to say. *Is it my fault? Is it hers?*

My questions are soon answered.

"Engelberta," he intones, voice soft but rolling with grief. "Is this what you've been doing?"

He approaches and stands over her hunched form like a disappointed father before his child.

"I'm sorry," she croaks, "I know I used fire."

"Not that." he says. "*This.*"

He gestures to the vines that wrap the crumbling village from its roots, to the earth walls that have crashed through house foundations.

To the dishevelled group of watching druids.

"It had to be done." she murmurs. "It had to be. We both know what happens when they do this, we both know..."

Her voice trails off into a barrage of shaking coughs.

Roth is beginning to look like a weight as large as a boulder is upon him. He reaches for her blackened hand.

"I'm sorry." he rumbles. "I've been searching for the higher powers for so long. I didn't realise you were still hurting."

She is silent. Only the tear tracks on her face remain.

"But I'd never suspected that you'd do this."

He glances back at me again.

"Kestra, yes?"

My heart jolts. I nod.

"Has anyone died here?"

That sickness sweeps through me again.

"I don't know." I gulp out. "Two of ours are... gone, but—"

"All right." he murmurs. Then he raises his deep voice, calling out to all who can hear:

"These people are not our enemies. We must repay them for this crime we have committed against them."

We, he said. *He too feels responsible.* Though his emotions seem to show on his face, there is still something deeply enigmatic about him. Despite his agelessness, he's like an old tree. Perhaps older than any even in the Duskwood.

Matthias calls out from the group, trapped beneath the vines the others used to restrain him:

"But they seek to destroy Duskwood!" he shouts weakly. Renate fixes him with a glare.

"Do we not also fell trees, when we must?" Roth calls to him. "Can we not even attempt to come together, to speak, and compromise? There are some things we will not stand for," his eyes drift to me and the scorch marks surrounding us, "but in the Oakfather's good name, this is not the answer."

Engelberta coughs again. And again. It does not stop.

Not this time.

We all know she's dying. Roth likely knew before all of us. I try to imagine it: a young, grieving Engelberta—and Roth, looking exactly as he does now, teaching her the Oakfather's way, completely unaware how much she would make it her own.

I see why he feels such fault. Someone like him should have seen it, should have tried to protect against it.

He beckons for the group to gather with an authority that everyone seems to understand intuitively. Tentatively, we all obey, eyeing each other with new uneasiness.

We were family. We were enemies.

I don't know what we are now.

Engelberta's sputtering coughs stop for a fleeting moment and she looks up at Roth with a strange peace. It will soon be the end—she's barely holding on, and she knows it. Her burnt body won't be able to take much more.

"We will perform the last rites," Roth rumbles. "Do you have any words to leave with us?"

"I..." she looks up at him, and then all of us. Her eyes avoid mine. Through coughs, she croaks: "I suppose I must apologise... for placing this burden on you all."

Conrad, propped up by Renate, locks eyes with her. *He's waiting for something. Anything.*

She just stares at him sadly.

Then her gaze returns to Roth.

"The sea," she croaks. "Voss, before they died. They always loved the sea. May I go into the next life the way they would have wanted to."

Voss. The sibling she lost?

As someone who tasted salt in the air from birth, I can't imagine loving the sea like that. But I suppose to someone who toiled in the belly of an ever-smoking factory, the sea was an escape. In the salt winds lay a song of hope.

So we all trudge to the beach. Roth supports Engelberta as she hobbles forth.

Conrad stays behind, alongside Renate and some of the other druids. I would have, too. I should have. She did terrible things. She made me live in fear. She wanted to take my first family from me, and turn my second against me.

And yet I go.

23

ENGELBERTA IS RETURNED PEACEFULLY to the earth, in view of the sea. Roth makes her one with the world under his fingertips —she crumbles away under his hand, and then she is gone.

What's left of her goes with the wind.

I don't cry. I just sink to the ground, exhaustion folding over me like a warm blanket.

Is it over?

My shoulder hurts. My skin aches with the burns and bruises she left on me. With a heaving sigh, my consciousness goes like she did into darkness, taken by the soft call of the sea.

24

It's been two weeks since Engelberta died.

I don't dwell on it. There are things to do in the here and now.

I'm sitting on a bench. The sea wind greets me. It isn't as cold as usual; Spring is here once again, and new birdsong flutters through the air. Beneath it rolls the sound of thudding hammers and light chatter. Hanshen is spread out behind me. Everything is moving—there's a scent of possibility around us all.

Apparently, I slept for a long time after everything ended. It was mostly exhaustion—Roth told me it was because I fought so much, and transformed into something powerful: something I'd never tried before.

My shoulder was only dislocated, though bruises and burns did cover much of my skin. I woke to find Renate by my bed—we had taken up in one of the unruined houses with the village council's permission.

That's what surprised me the most.

She told me that once the chaos was done, she approached the evacuees on the beach. Though some villagers were badly injured, the consensus was that no one was dead—yet.

After pledging to help them, there was protest from some. The druids had caused this situation, after all. It was the instinctual opinion of a good chunk of Hanshen that we should leave immediately, or live in fear of their wrath. Then Florian stepped in, alongside many of those whose families had been saved before their eyes. After understanding from Renate that this was a three-sided battle, it was easier to coax the villagers into accepting help—despite the strange magic they saw from us.

Florian was clever about it. He had Renate manipulate some sea water for the ones who still felt the tug of the Speaker's old views—for how could someone granted power over the sea be an enemy of Rhene? This seemed to set everything up for a tentative alliance. Now, as the sound of building and chatter catches on the sea wind, I think there might be hope.

Perhaps each side is realising that the other is made up of people, too.

During one of the days when I was still relegated to bed, Roth came to visit. I can still remember his stern expression in the twilight of my dark room, the lines in his face as he eyed my burns.

"Do you feel able to produce some flame?" he asked.

Heart beating fast with a sudden fear, I nodded weakly. My mind ran wild—was this it? After everything, would I die now to Roth?

When I created it, I held it carefully in my hand. It lit the dusky room with a warmth that I now recognise as my own.

"How does your hand feel?"

"Fine." I replied. "Why?"

"Interesting." he rumbled. "I didn't believe it could be done without intensive training."

I stared blankly, waiting for him to go on.

"As you probably observed, Engelberta's fire burnt her beyond belief," he elaborated, "but here you sit with yours as though you're simply holding a warm stone. Strange indeed."

Fire destroys. That precept echoed in my mind.

"Oh. That's why..." I breathe. Roth nodded.

"I advise against learning it because it normally hurts the user. It seems that Engelberta built on that in her own way, reading things in it that weren't there."

He sighed, then continued:

"Because of who she was. Because of what she knew of life."

"So you're not going to—" I blurted. Roth waved a hand dismissively at the idea of any punishment, turning to the door.

"You have a gift, Kestra. I see that now."

He opened it with a creak. *He'll have to duck to get through,* I thought amusedly. Then he paused.

"Though that does not mean you should not continue to learn, whether by yourself or from me. The offer is open."

Then he was gone.

A shift in the breeze coaxes me from my thoughts again. I haven't seen Roth around since then. It's probably wise of him to stay away—the villagers seem able to handle druids that look and sound like them, but there's no telling what kind of unease Roth's antlered, winged presence would bring. I find his appearance soothing, though. He looks strange, but there's something calming about him, full of quiet wisdom.

But they don't know him as that person. *Though perhaps one day they will.*

The breeze turns again.

Strange.

I glance to the side and spy Liesl, strolling tentatively towards me. She sits down without a word.

I want to say something. Anything. For the past two weeks, she's avoided me as though I'm diseased.

But nothing comes to me. We just stare at the sea together.

"Mother's coming round to it all." she says.

"What?"

"You. Them." She takes a long, slow breath. "Me. Though I haven't told her yet."

I remain silent. A single word on this subject feels like it could be fatal. Seeing my nervousness, she speaks again:

"I think I always knew I was..." She trails off.

"Different." I supply, with a bittersweet quirk of my mouth. She nods.

"But I couldn't be headstrong the way you were. I saw how Mother treated you. All I ever wanted was her approval. If she'd said those horrible things to me, I don't think I would have wanted to be alive anymore."

I see it in her eyes—the bright terror. She remembers that screaming panic of that day. She remembers the fire that blazed within our unhappy home.

"Tell her when you're ready," I say, "but if you want to learn more, I think I know someone who might understand."

The sea wind echoes between us.

Before I know it, she's slid up the bench and has put her arms around me. I acquiesce, falling exhaustedly into the sudden embrace.

I don't think we've ever hugged before. It's nice. The way she smells reminds me of home. There's a welling up in my heart, and I notice my eyes are wet.

"Thank you," she whispers.

In response, I hug her tighter.

More weeks pass. Hanshen is beginning to look like it did when I first flew over it on the dawn of the attack. Some druids have even begun to make themselves at home—particularly Otto. His cooking is as irresistible to the villagers as it is to me—understandable, considering that they're people who have lived primarily on bland fish stew their entire lives.

During my recovery time, I sat in on a few village meetings. Florian has been true to his word: every person that has reached adulthood is now allowed a vote on important village issues. Seeing the way he speaks sparks a hopeful sensation in my chest. His mannerisms, his cadence, everything—his practice from telling so many stories has given him a magnetism in speech that brings people together. If not in opinion, then in the agreement that the discussions themselves should be had.

Things are looking bright. But something tugs at my bones. Whenever I stare out at the Rhenesee, I can't help but think of what's beyond it. The dreams of flame and ruin are gone now, but the bright cities have returned, stronger than ever.

Renate feels it too—we have to leave. She wants to go home. And wherever she goes, I will go. There's no question of it. Our old plan, to go to Brennof and catch a ship to Cer'ah, still shines bright in my mind. Hanshen is getting better, but it's still in the process of growing, in more ways than one. And I can't stay here forever, anyway.

I can't go back to the church now either—it wouldn't feel right. I'd see Engelberta's ghost wherever I walked.

So one bright dawn, laden with supplies, we walk to Hanshen's gates. Florian is there, full of hugs and encouraging words. He understands this; he understands me. He always has.

Otto, truly settled in, gives us a warm nod. He stands by the side of a village woman I can't remember the name of—nevertheless, they look happy.

Ari, Leot and Ilse are ever the trio. They'll be returning to the church soon after we leave, I've heard, ready to learn more and change the old ways. Embraces and goodbyes are shared between us, with many tears in Ari's case.

It's all so bittersweet—but so beautiful, too. To be known. To be loved.

I even see my mother at the gates. We haven't spoken, but there's a tide of understanding between us. Perhaps one day we will speak, as truly different people.

I've been growing, but it seems she still has some to do before we can begin to properly understand each other. Liesl nods from her side, and waves tentatively as we go. She'll grow, too—I introduced her to Roth. One day, perhaps, she might stand where I stood.

There's one person that brings tears to my eyes in his goodbye. A late riser, as always, Conrad runs up to us frantically and hugs us both, pulling us down with a desperate, loving strength. His burn is healing well—Renate's water seems to soothe it in a way we can't quite understand. Soon the scar may be a faint memory —a mere shadow on the side of his face.

"Thank you." he says. "You both mean more to me than you can ever know."

After Engelberta's death, he turned in on himself. Though he helped with the rebuilding efforts, there was something ghost-like about him. All comfort seemed to slide from him like water. In recent weeks, though, I've seen a fire begin to burn. He's brighter. He walks like he knows what he has to do.

As we all stand in this crooked, loving embrace, he explains:

"I'm going back to the church with the others. I'll learn, and learn, and learn. Once Roth has nothing more to teach me, I'm going to find her. My mother." His voice cracks a little on the last word. "I know she's out there."

He sniffs, breathing through the tears, and hugs us tighter. My face is wet, too, and my heart is glowing with a gentle ache. I hope he finds what he's looking for. And I hope that, in time, he makes peace with the ghost of the mother he once had.

With our goodbyes done, we turn to leave. From the crowd comes a young voice. I recognise its owner—one of the young men whose family Renate saved.

"My offer of marriage still stands, Renate!"

Renate looks back and chuckles. Then she takes me by the hand and kisses me. It's warm, like spring rain. It feels right. When she breaks away, I'm chuckling too. With happiness. With hope.

I'll go anywhere with her—I've known that for a while. Now everyone else knows it too.

Without waiting to see everyone's reactions, we fold into ourselves and take off—Renate as her beautiful blue-tinged eagle, and me with the golden eyes I can't seem to shake off.

I distantly glimpse Roth watching us from Duskwood's faraway treeline. His distinct silhouette lies rooted like an old oak.

Everything will be alright here.

The future spreads out like a green, living tapestry ahead of us. Duskwood is learning the song of Spring again. In the very far distance lie the silhouettes of each Spire, waiting with rocky wisdom to guide us into the land beyond—and then even farther, to the rest of the world.

I hear it calling. Now is the time to fly.

EPILOGUE

Brennof bustles with people and scents, of food and smoke and salt. There are sounds everywhere, too. The crashing of the waves is muffled by constant chatter, in every language I ever knew existed and more. Traders call alongside greedy gulls, fighting over who can be the loudest. Multitudes of people come and go like shadows, there and then not. Pillars of smoke rise in the distance.

She comes to my mind again. *The dead woman. The grey bird.* I shake her out.

We stand before the gangplank of a passenger boat, headed for Cer'ah. Passage is fairly cheap, as long as we don't want any kind of luxury. I don't mind it—being here with Renate is enough.

She stands in front of me in the line, dark hair constantly ruffled by the wind. The sun glimmers on her skin like it's formed of bronze, and her light tunic flows like a waterfall in the breeze. Before us, past the dock and the people and the ship, lies the Hallesee, bluer than any I've imagined. At home, the sea was more often grey, but here the sun glints off it like it's filled with rich sapphires.

The line moves, and we all shuffle forward. As I stare out at the coastline, I vaguely hear Renate give her name to a crew member, who's noting us all down as we pass.

"No last name?" he enquires.

"Just Renate, for now." she replies, and boards the boat.

I worried about her fear—the last time she set foot on one of these, it ended in tragedy. But now there's a strong grace to her movements. She doesn't need to fear. She is master of the water.

He turns to me, next in line.

"Name?"

"Kestra."

I see him open his mouth to ask for a last name. Before he can speak, I answer. It feels like the simplest thing I've ever done. Who I am, everything that's happened to me—I will take the name they gave me, and all that came with it.

"Duskwood." I say. "My name is Kestra Duskwood."

REVIEWS

If you enjoyed this book, please consider leaving me a review on Amazon, Bookbub, or Goodreads. Just a rating or a line is fine. They really make a huge impact for authors.

ACKNOWLEDGMENTS

Firstly: Argonauts, Marine Biologists, Dad-Killers United, etc. Thank you for those three wonderful years of playing Kestra Duskwood—from a wandering, drunken druid to a near-immortal guardian of the last world tree. From a loner to a loved companion. As the chicken once said: what is joy really if there's no one to share it with?

Thanks as well to everyone who genuinely loves and supports what I do—whether it be music, art or, more topically, writing. I can't seem to stop creating things, so don't worry—you're not going to run out.

For updates, visit my website: **www.awolf.uk**

Printed in Great Britain
by Amazon